THE HOMECOMING GAME

THE
HOMECOMING GAME

a novel by Howard Nemerov

afterword by Albert Lebowitz

UNIVERSITY OF MISSOURI PRESS / COLUMBIA AND LONDON

Copyright © 1957, 1985 by Howard Nemerov
Originally published by Simon and Schuster
First Missouri printing, 1992
Afterword copyright © 1992 by
The Curators of the University of Missouri
University of Missouri Press, Columbia, Missouri 65201
Printed and bound in the United States of America
5 4 3 2 1   96 95 94 93 92

Library of Congress Cataloging–in–Publication Data

Nemerov, Howard.
    The homecoming game : a novel / by Howard Nemerov ;
afterword by Albert Lebowitz.
        p.   cm.
    ISBN 0–8262–0870–3 (paper)
    I. Title.
    PS3527.E5H6   1992
    813′.54—dc20   92–15687
                                                         CIP

∞™ This paper meets the requirements of the
American National Standard for Permanence of Paper
for Printed Library Materials, Z39.48, 1984.

to Peggy

The author wishes to acknowledge his gratitude to the Editors of the Kenyon Review *for their grant of a Fellowship in 1955, which was of assistance in the composition of this book.*

THE HOMECOMING GAME

1

Mr. Charles Osman, speaking in his customary abstracted and precise manner, which came through to the young ladies and gentlemen of his class as a parody of the pedantic style, something sarcastically or hopelessly conscious of itself and of everything else in the world, began to gather together his books and papers while still talking, a sign that he had reached his peroration.

"Of numerous views as to what the study of history is, or what the study of history is for," he was saying, "I happen to hold, as you know, with the one which contends that the historian examines the outsides of past events, with a view to discovering what their insides were. Regarded in this rather cold light, most histories are the failure of history, and this that we have been considering this morning is one such. No one, so far as I am aware, has succeeded in viewing the inside of the fool, or villain, or fool and villain, called Titus Oates, who brought the realm of Albion to such great confusion, who was whipped through Tyburn— the whipping evidently designed by those in authority to be fatal, but it was not—and who then, with a change in administration, as we should call it, was rewarded with a royal pension of four hundred pounds per annum, on which he lived a retired life to a good old age. If his story, and that of the Popish Plot altogether, remind us of certain events in the recent past of our own land, and seem to give us a momentary penetration, among all those parading kings and noblemen, into some enduring realities on the human scene, realities pre-eminently illuminated by folly and villainy, we shall be perhaps not far off the point, though we make the comparison, as some say, at our peril."

The eleven o'clock bell began to strike during the last sentence, a dramatic exactitude appreciated by the students, who tended to see in it not an academic facility so much as a striking feat of teaching technique developed out of consideration for themselves. Ordinarily, Mr. Osman would have finished his last sentence while on his way to the door, a great discouragement to those who habitually ask questions after the hour, but this morning he sat quite still watching the class

4

break into quiet disorder and leave. Particularly he watched a young man by the name of Raymond Blent, who was aware of being watched; their eyes met for a steady instant before the student turned away and went through the door. Charles Osman made his own gaze as neutral and expressionless as possible, and felt disappointed at seeing the same gaze returned, yet at the same time somewhat relieved that the young man's face expressed neither sullenness nor self-pity.

He has clearly been given an opportunity to speak up, Charles thought; was it possible after all that no one was going to make a fuss? As a person accustomed to the close inspection of his own thoughts and feelings, he observed in himself a slight disappointment at the idea that the smooth waters of rule and routine were about to close over an event which might have produced a view of certain realities. He sighed.

"For such disappointments," he said aloud to the empty disorder of chairs, "we should always be grateful."

"Did you speak to us, sir?" The voice, somewhat more respectful than was necessary, came from the open door, where there now appeared two students. One of these, Mr. Arthur Barber, known to Charles as the president of the Student Council, came forward into the room, while the other lingered at the door like, Charles thought, a bodyguard. Young Mr. Barber was smiling with friendly confidence, a man known and loved by all the people, as it were, a boy who had never been turned down.

"No, I wasn't," Charles said. "Teachers habitually

talk to themselves, Mr. Barber; it is a vocational disease."

"Ah, I didn't know you knew who I was," said Barber, evidently pleased and advancing with open hand, which Charles, rising, shook somewhat reluctantly; it seemed to him that by knowing the name he had already conceded something to the boy's opinion of himself.

"I'm pleased, of course," Barber said, "and of course I know who you are, sir. I've heard splendid things about your courses, and regret my own studies have prevented me from learning at your feet."

Charles, who was standing at this time, looked doubtfully at his feet.

"An expression," said Barber, and turned to the other boy. "This is Lou da Silva," he said, "on the student honor committee. Lou, this is Professor Osman."

"How do you do," said Charles with a polite smile to the other boy, who merely nodded, however, and remained by the door. So! Charles thought. There is to be a fuss after all. One might have known.

"We don't want to interrupt you if you're busy, sir," Barber said, looking around the room as though to emphasize that this form of words, under the circumstances, was a form of words. "We could come back another time. But if you could spare us a few minutes?"

"Glad to," Charles said. "Speak your piece, gentlemen."

"Piece?" Barber asked, with a slightly pained look.

"An expression," Charles said.

"I hope you don't think, or won't think," Barber began, "that we're lacking in respect for the faculty, or for you personally, if I say right off that we are here to ask if you won't reconsider a certain recent decision of yours—a decision which naturally you had every right to make, no one questions that—a decision about one of our fellow students individually, yes, but through him, you see, a decision which affects everyone on campus."

Barber spoke this prologue in a candid and serious way, his eyes firmly fixed on Charles's eyes; indeed, everything about him bespoke, a little professionally, the candid and serious person, the responsible young man. He was rather stout, with a light complexion and fair hair already somewhat thin, and on this campus so largely given to dungarees, windbreakers and sports jackets of many colors he dressed generally in dark blue suits, as though giving already a prospective approval to the image of himself in twenty years' time. Even his being fat gave an impression of maturity; it was not so much a physical fact as an emblem of political solidity. Charles, warning himself against feelings of irritation—for this delegation was surely to have been expected, and he ought not in any case to make Barber the victim of his aversion from Barber's general type—nevertheless felt it was time for him to break up the young man's apparently deliberated approach and put him where he had to improvise.

"Mr. Barber," he said gently, "you are not addressing a meeting. I have a fair idea of your errand. It's about Raymond Blent, is it not? Why not say flatly what you want me to do, and then we'll see if it is possible for me to do it?"

"I'm sorry, sir," Barber said. "But you know how it is, for students talking to faculty—I guess I've turned the whole thing over in my mind so many times since last night that it came out like a speech." To Charles, this revealed a candor somewhat behind and beneath the political candor of the surface, and he smiled.

"You probably don't care much about football, sir," Barber said. "And I can appreciate that some people foolishly overestimate its importance."

"But I do," said Charles, "care about football, that is. I go to every game we play at home."

"Then you know about Ray Blent, about what he means to us here?"

"I do," Charles said.

"Well, we thought it might be possible, sir, for us to work out some other solution to this situation that's developed, just at the last minute, with Blent." Barber broke off here, and for the first time his eyes failed to meet Charles's. Even in the fair flower of his innocence, thought Charles, he perceives that there is something rather enormous about the idea if it has to be spoken openly.

"Do you mean," he asked, "that I should simply take my notebook and change the F to a D—a B would be better, an F would change quite easily into a B in two strokes of the pen—so that Blent may play in the Homecoming Game?"

"I realize that what we're asking is a pretty big

8

thing, sir." Barber, hanging his head, appeared to consider seriously how big this thing was.

"You wouldn't have to go that far, maybe." Da Silva spoke up for the first time, and, as he spoke, closed the door of the room. "You might say you wanted to reconsider his exam, and then not give in the grade till Monday."

"Mr. da Silva," said Charles, "are you really on the student honor committee?"

"Yes, sir."

"Chairman, in fact," said Barber, giving, however, a warning backward look to the other boy.

"Well, dear me," said Charles.

"Now, Lou," said Barber, and added to Charles, "I know Lou didn't really mean to suggest you do anything off-beat of that kind. It's only that we were going over all the possibilities at our last night's meeting, and we naturally considered a great many silly solutions as well as sensible ones."

"You have devoted a meeting to this subject?"

"Well, sir," said Barber, "it was rather urgent business, since if anything can be done at all it must be done today. I know it's hard on you teachers that these November Hour Exams come during the football season; with a little sense the administration would schedule them a week or ten days later. But there it is—and here we are." An inclusive gesture of his hands made Charles and himself equally the victims of difficult fate.

"Things do sometimes happen the hard way, Mr. Barber," Charles said. "But I don't suppose you came here unprovided with some ethical solution? After all, the event is public now, the lists are up, the boy is ineligible. I imagine even the NCAA would be interested in any opportune reversal of that decision."

"Dr. Osman—" the title indicated to Charles that the big plea was now being launched—"if you look at the matter fairly and squarely, can you possibly see any extenuating circumstances for Blent's flunk in your course? I mean, for instance, that the boy is not just another dumb athlete—" the "boy"; it was very man-to-man now, Charles observed—"but on the whole, as a matter of fact, a pretty good student, with a pretty good record? Or that he may have been nervous and upset when he took your test? I mean, the Homecoming Game is a pretty big event in this boy's career, his last appearance in college football, the big test . . . and there's some chance, small as this place is, of his making All-American, the first one this college ever had. These things may not mean much to you, sir, I understand that—but we've got to consider them in trying to get the whole picture."

"Mr. Barber," said Charles, "it would be my view that you are going about this in a rather odd fashion. *We* are not being asked to get, or to interpret, the whole picture. I happen to have been hired for no reason other than to teach the history of England, which I am qualified to do. My judgments on the whole picture are so seldom solicited that I have got out of the habit of making them, perhaps. I sympathize with Blent, with you, with, Lord knows, everybody, and mostly with myself for being in this predicament. There are always extenuating circumstances; a third-string guard, who shall be nameless, also flunked my Hour Exam and is ineligible, but I very much doubt any appeal will be made in his behalf. You come here, I imagine, with the most kindly intentions imaginable, but please, even with the most kindly intentions imaginable, do not slip into the conversational habit of saying 'we' when you are speaking of my decisions."

"I'm sorry, sir," said Barber, in a tone and with a glance expressive of a number of feelings, none of them sorrow. It was clear that he was not accustomed to being spoken to in this way, and Charles felt that he had made his remarks somewhat stronger, or more personal, than necessary.

"I grant you," he added more quietly, "that it's too bad this has happened at all, and worse that it has happened at a time which brings out all the situation's potential of cheap melodrama. But really, you must not begin, Barber, by losing your head and implying that it is somehow my fault."

"There is something, sir, about that." Barber now spoke rather confidentially. "I suppose you know, sir, that you've got quite a reputation here as a ferocious man with a grade? I mean," he hastily added, holding up his hand, "that's a good thing, as a rule. I've always said that if there's one thing this place needs, it's a certain intellectual dignity; and people who take courses with you know before the first week is over that they're in for a truly educational experience. And they like you for it, and respect you for it."

"Good of them," observed Charles.

"At the same time, there's a general feeling that you've got to temper the wind a little bit now and again, isn't there? And this football business is a pretty delicate matter—you know how much trouble there's been over it in the past years, about overemphasis and de-emphasis, and all that. We thought—we on the Student Council, I mean, and our faculty and administration advisers—that we had all that straightened out now, in a way satisfactory to all concerned, all except the football-crazy on the one hand and, on the other, those die-hard faculty members who won't allow any value to football whatsoever. We thought we had the situation pretty well under control; that football had its legitimate place in the scheme of things, that the academic side was sufficiently protected by rules, et cetera, et cetera. Why, the team even has its own tutor, to keep the boys up in their studies, and you must admit, Dr. Osman, that one reason Blent failed your exam was that he has such a good record that Coach Hardy excused him from tutoring sessions; in a way, you might say he failed just because he was a good student, taking things by and large."

Charles had to smile at this.

"Barber, you do seem to have some philosophical talents, don't you?" he said. "What do you suggest, then, practically speaking?"

"Give the lad another chance," Barber said, somewhat urgently. "Let him take a make-up exam today, and then, well, sir, if I were you—if I were you, I'd forget to correct that exam until Monday."

12

"In your opinion, Mr. Barber, I should be absolutely honest in playing it that way?"

Barber looked as suspicious as possible to his comfortable nature.

"Absolutely honest, sir?" he said. "Well, if you put it to me, I can only say that I think it the right thing to do under the circumstances. And the generous thing."

"So that I should be right and generous all weekend and absolutely honest starting, say, on Monday morning?"

Charles, who was losing his temper, spoke so evenly that Barber, taking in rather the gentle tone than the sense of these words, had started to nod his head in agreement before the sentence ended. Now his benign expression became overspread with one of dismayed anger.

"Knock it off, Arthur," said Da Silva, who came forward, a small, wiry person with black hair and a very aggressive stance.

"The kid's too honest to live," he said to Charles. "I'd just like to know, once and for all, are you going to give the hero a break or not? Yes or no?"

This speech was for Charles a new insight into campus politics, and it made him nervous.

"Your approach is more attractive than his," he said to Da Silva with a smile which was with great definiteness not returned. "Are you threatening me?"

"You could look pretty bad, you and your honesty," Da Silva said.

"Now, Lou, that's not the way," Barber began.

"You trying to get something back on the boy," said

Da Silva, "or what?" He smiled now, with an effect of cynical connivance. "Why not help out and flannel things over, Mr. Osman? You know it's what everybody wants. You know this isn't just a couple of crummy students pleading for their crummy classmate—there's force behind this, you know that, don't you? If you don't do the right thing by us, it all starts up the line, to the higher echelons, and by tonight your hair will be full of deans, and alumni will be coming out your ears —and for what? Make it easy, please, Mr. Osman, won't you?"

"I don't doubt, Mr. da Silva," said Charles, "that you are ready to make me all the trouble you can—and, as you say, for what? It's hard to believe you are serious— either of you. As for your last speech, Mr. da Silva, you surely must see that if I had any remote notion of going along with your wishes, you have made it impossible for me to do so.

"Let me say a word to both you gentlemen: your technique is bad. In your different ways, you are equally of the type which sees all things as political, and it could not have occurred to your typically limited intelligence that Mr. Blent, having two legs and a brain, might have come to me himself about his problem but did not. Instead, you lost no time in making the matter your business and holding a meeting about it. What might have been settled decently between a student and his teacher becomes at once, in your hands, an occasion for the exercise of your thinly disguised hostilities, and for a cheap display of what you doubtless consider to be power, for which, I am glad to tell you,

I have some contempt. Are you quite clear on that point? Then you may go."

"Okay, if that's the way you want it," said Da Silva, retiring to the door. Barber, however, lingered at the desk.

"I want you to understand, sir," he said with dignity, "that Lou is speaking for himself. No one wants to pressure you into anything against your conscience, or threaten you, or anything like that—I certainly don't agree with Lou there. You are responsible, after all, for your own decisions, and I hope you never see occasion to regret them."

"All right, Arthur," said Da Silva from the door. "Arthur is a nice fellow," he said to Charles, "only there's something sneaky in his nature, don't you think so?" and he smiled at Charles in a relatively friendly way. "You're on your own," he added, as they both disappeared.

2

The lecture-halls, dormitories, and administrative buildings of the College were arranged around a green called the Oval. Charles, emerging from Lemuel Hall, decided against proceeding at once to Ambry Hall just next door, where he would pick up his mail; instead he walked slowly the other way, around the driveway which formed the perimeter of the Oval, with an idea of cooling off before facing the next thing, whatever that might be.

The new class hour had already, of course, begun, and the Oval was deserted; it never failed to strike

Charles as vaguely remarkable that on the stroke of each bell through the day some fifteen hundred people suddenly appeared, filling this quiet space with the murmur of their migration from one province of knowledge to the next, and, as suddenly, ten minutes later, were gone; disposed according to a highly abstract order some hundreds of years old which had precipitated out in gray fieldstone and red brick its material equivalent (the philosophy building, the English literature building, the chemistry building, and so forth), just as though these names and divisions and buildings referred to some real and eternal distinction in the nature of things as well as the nature of knowledge about things. Order, order of any sort, and merely considered in itself, was no doubt a wonderful thing.

The day had begun splendidly, as autumn days regularly did here, with a brilliant frost on the grass, an air strange and keen in the mouth as the first taste of an apple; now, however, it was beginning to lose its character. The grass glistened as commonly as in spring, only a few white frost shadows lay along the ground, people's noses no doubt were beginning to run; it was too warm. Charles took off his overcoat and slung it across his shoulder with the green book-bag which on this campus had a strange snob appeal as the casual sign of a large and ancient university in the East, where such things were the fashion. He walked slowly around the Oval, arriving at his destination by the longest route, and considered his feelings about the mean little interview in which he had just been caught; these feelings were such as did credit to a civilized man—they were mixed.

There was, first, his indignation, which increased upon the consideration that he had to suffer whatever of it remained undelivered to those two students, whose heads, at this instant, he would gladly have knocked together. Didn't they know, didn't they even suspect by this time, that one simply didn't talk to people as they had talked to him? That what their being in such a place as this implied was, in the first place, their will to civilization, civilization with all its admitted faults and evils, civilization at all costs? But their morals, no less than their manners, belonged in a reformatory, not in a university. (The College was not a university, so Charles, in moments of high feeling, used the term to express a fine scorn for all that was not civilization.)

But by a process of induction familiar to all articulate persons—whereby whenever we take up an unequivocal position or make a firm stand its opposite at once begins to look attractive, and even right—he felt doubt, anxiety, disgust, and even, a little, fear.

For clearly he had been betrayed by the heat and immediacy of the time into an attitude more positive and definite than he had intended, by himself, to take. On the one hand, there could not have been any question of his not failing Blent, for the boy's examination admitted no question; it was merely atrocious. On the other hand, Charles resented, hated, even, the implication that he belonged to that rigorously formalist class of instructors whose view of the teacher's function was

17

inflexibly narrow and mechanical; nor for that matter did he dislike football. Had Blent but come to him with some halfway plausible excuse—Charles had hoped he would—or had he so much as said in extenuation, "I'm sorry about your test. I was worried about other things," Charles believed he would have found the boy a way out, moral positions be damned. There would still, even now, be time and room for maneuver, had not those two officious donkeys thrust their way into the matter, making his statement that "you can't do it this way" so forceful that to all intents it became "you can't do it at all."

At the same time, the dramatic sense of "a situation" somewhat exhilarated him; in several years at this institution he had kept his nose clean, as they say, having seen examples in some plenty of dishonesty and cheap behavior but nothing which he considered either sufficiently crucial or sufficiently close to himself to demand any stern action on his part. Now there probably would be trouble—probably less, though, than those undergraduates optimistically thought of making—and Charles, acknowledging a touch of nervous fear, saw nevertheless with pleasure that the fear did not refer to externals, to his security or anything anyone could do to him, but to the internal and problematic; it was a natural fear, perhaps, of going through all the anticipated effort and strain only to make, when it was too late, the discovery that one had been quite simply mistaken, that there was no issue, that one had been wrong and suffered some inexpensive martyrdom foolishly. His knowledge of the world, his professional view of history for that matter, amply gave him instances of clowns who walked the high wire of the ethical; the laughs would be loudest when they broke their necks. Despite all that, though, the idea of a crisis somewhat inspired him against his judgment; it appeared to define, though dimly as yet, some differences and discontents he had entertained for a number of years against this institution of higher learning in which he worked, and against whatever it might be that this institution stood for in most generalized form, as well as against what he thought of as the mediocrity, or at least the superficiality, of virtue.

Such considerations as these brought Charles around the Oval to Ambry Hall.

As he went down the hall to his mailbox he was summoned by Mrs. Feuermann, the departmental secretary.

"President Nagel's compliments," this lady said sweetly, "and will Mr. Osman, if he is free, step round to the president's office just at noon? I told him you had nothing scheduled," she added.

"How helpful can one be?" said Charles, scowling; and she laughed.

"I'm told they're thinking of starting you at fullback," she said, "and a fine figure of a man you'd be, too, in your moleskins."

"If they send my head back in a box," Charles said, "mail it to Mother. It didn't take you long," he added, "to get the gist of what is going on."

"We girls and our telephones," said Mrs. Feuermann merrily. "Meanwhile a student is waiting to see you, a Miss Sayre. I've put her in the large conference room."

"I don't know a Miss Sayre," Charles said grumpily. "Everyone is getting in on the act."

"Mr. Blent's intended, dear," said Mrs. Feuermann. "She is how you say *pinned to him.*"

In his mailbox Charles found the usual circulars beginning, e.g., "Dear Professor: Would you like to know how your colleagues have received our new text, *History for the Young in Heart?*" A national magazine advertised "up-to-the-minute quizzes on current events," and added that because the editors knew teachers were often too busy to do *all* the reading necessary for understanding the modern world, a free answer sheet would be sent in plain wrapper with every ten subscriptions.

The nearest wastebasket was some steps away, down the hall, and as Charles moved toward it with this stuff in his hands he passed the office of Dr. Lestrange, head of the department.

"Charley," came that booming voice through the open door.

"Busy," Charles replied, dumping the mail in the basket. "Student to see."

"One word, only take a minute." The voice was jovial but peremptory, and Charles obeyed.

Lestrange was a gigantic old man with a high complexion and wild white hair who had once been an All-American tackle at some Southern school.

"Come right to the point, don't want to waste your time," he cried when Charles stood in the doorway (a trifle deaf, he never spoke in conversational tones and when he taught had to have an empty classroom on either side of his own). "Run the boy, Charley. Don't stand in his way. My advice."

"Well, sir . . ." Charles felt uncertain how to meet anything this blunt.

"No damn morality involved," shouted Dr. Lestrange. "Not pulling my rank. Only my advice to you, son. Why fuss? Beautiful broken field runner, that kid—give me one more chance to watch him. I love to see the boy.

"Anyhow," he added in a mere roar meant to indicate confidential communication, "what do you think this is, an institution of higher learning? In a mass of nincompoops like this a good back is an educational achievement. Let the boy run, what the hell?"

"Ah," Charles said noncommittally as he turned away. "Thanks, Henry, I'd like to."

"Not trying to pressure you," came that huge voice down the hall behind him. "Do what you damn please, I'm standing behind you. But I'd like to see the boy go, though."

That last piece of amplified wistfulness echoing in the corridor touched Charles; it seemed to him that Lestrange was quite right.

There at any rate is an honest man, he thought as he opened the door of the conference room.

This room, where the History Department held its weekly meeting, had always depressed Charles. High-ceilinged and on the whole pleasant in its proportions, it was nonetheless all wrong; it had, a doctor would say, a bad history. The wainscoting of dark wood, the wall-covering above that which seemed made of stained straw, the long, cracked, chipped table surrounded with

21

alertly waiting chairs; above this the ghostly white glass bowl of the chandelier hung on a heavy chain from a white ceiling molded in complex and repetitive forms— all this seemed to him the essence of much in academic life, which, striving for a serious austerity, achieved shabbiness. Because the room blindingly faced the sun during most of the day, the shades had been left drawn, and the light, what there was, hung in a yellowish brown fog over the reflecting lake of that long table. Dust danced in the light at the edges of the shades; it all smelled dully of ink, chalk, and, one might fancy, the sweat of impatience too long controlled.

The student stood near the window, and turned toward him at his entrance; he could not make out much about her in that light save that her hair was pale blond or so. She was smoking a cigarette, and a fur coat was sprawled like a dead brown animal across the table.

"Miss Sayre?" Charles said.

"Lily Sayre." She came round the table and, like Barber earlier, more or less forced him to shake hands. At the same time, thought Charles, you had to allow she was prettier than Barber. She had a thin, serious, intelligent face, a trifle too long, maybe, and a pale, lucid complexion; her hair fell loose to her shoulders in an artistic arrangement suggesting natural freedom, even wildness. She wore a blue denim skirt—not pants, at any rate—and a man's white shirt (Charles noted it was clean) open at the throat, where a rope of pearls was knotted roughly and even violently.

"What can I do for you, Miss Sayre?"

"Most likely very little, I don't know," she said. "Are you a man of sense?"

"A what?"

"A man of sense, *honnête homme.* It's a French idea."

"So I gather," Charles said gently.

"Well, it is," she insisted, "and you needn't look as if you were trying not to laugh. It's a serious question."

"And very learnedly expressed."

"What I mean is," the girl said, "are you like, say, Count Mosca in the *Chartreuse?*"

"I wouldn't have thought so, no," Charles replied. "But I was about your age when I read it last, maybe I've improved since. And if I were, you wouldn't expect me to admit it. Suppose you simply tell me what you want, and decide about my character later?"

"A student feels at a disadvantage talking to a faculty member," said Lily Sayre. "Faculty members are so used to being right. I'd hoped we might start on a different footing."

She now stubbed out her cigarette on the conference table, watching him meanwhile as though to test him by his response to this trivial liberty.

"I want to talk to you sort of personally," she said, and added, with what Charles thought admirable self-possession, "I don't imagine anything in your contract requires you to listen to that from a student."

"But I am listening," Charles said. "You want to talk about Raymond Blent."

"Yes, I do, but please don't get the idea that I've come to put pressure on you—"

"You couldn't," Charles said abruptly, fixing her with a stare which she returned. "No one could."

"No, I don't suppose anyone could," she said after a moment, and smiled. "It's only that my father is a trustee here, and I *have* occasionally been called a spoiled brat—which might be true—so I wanted to say right off that you needn't hear me unless you want to."

"That's fair of you," Charles observed. "You rely on my curiosity."

"On that," she answered, "and on my being a girl talking to a man—I rely on everything available, naturally."

"I'm willing to hear what you have to say," he returned, "but I should let you know first that the position has become somewhat embattled already; what the educators call 'broader issues' are involved."

"They would be, wouldn't they?" Lily said with a little sigh. "No one is ever personal any more. People don't even get mad at other people, they get mad at other people's principles."

"People die of it all the same," said Charles. "But that's not what you wanted to talk about." He looked at his watch. "The great battle of principles begins in twenty minutes, so you'd better say what you have to say."

"It's a little long and involved," she said, "but it all belongs together, even if I seem to start a long way back, so please don't interrupt."

She turned away to get a cigarette from the coat on the table, and offered him one and even lit it for him.

After they had solemnly puffed smoke at one another for a moment, she began.

"I sing, essentially, the dreary wrath of Achilles," was her somewhat odd opening, "Achilles who sulks in the locker room."

Charles found her voice delightfully cool and dark in these phrases; nevertheless he said, "Without the allegory, Miss Sayre, if you don't mind."

"You're right," she said. "I had it all very elaborately worked out before I came, because it embarrasses me to have to talk so much about myself. I was to be Briseis, and Daddy was Agamemnon—but never mind. I also thought it would charm you professionally if I were a bit blue-stocking.

"Anyhow, without false modesty, I am pretty, or handsome, without being any great beauty. I'm fairly witty and I'm also quite rich. My mother died when I was a child, and my father had to travel a good deal, so I went from school to school, mostly in Europe. That's why I'm a couple of years older than my classmates here, and that's why there's a kind of erotic snob appeal about me which gets me into these odd situations.

"Because I am all Daddy has in the world outside of a railroad and some hotels and so forth, I agreed to come here to his Alma Mater and behave as much as possible like an American undergraduate, even though I don't really believe I'm fooling anyone."

What an extraordinarily assured young woman, Charles thought. Erotic snob appeal, forsooth.

"Now, enter Achilles." She stopped, smiled, and said,

"No, I must drop Achilles. But I want to tell this to you very coldly, and not making excuses for myself."

"Are you sure you want to tell me at all," asked Charles, "if you are engaged to the boy?"

"Not engaged—pinned; something altogether more adolescent and tribal than an engagement. I am, or I was, part of Ray's reputation with his fraternity brothers. It happened quite suddenly about mid-season; everything, you see, is dated by football games. There had been a hundred-and-three-yard, or maybe it was a hundred-and-four-yard, return of a kick-off, which pleased everyone a great deal. Ray was pleased with himself, I was pleased that he was pleased—at this time he had taken me out a few times, nothing more—and his fraternity brothers were, oh, terribly pleased. They made much of him at a party, and much of me for sort of being attached to him. There's nothing much to be done with Ray at a party except make much of him, because he is in training and doesn't drink; but I sometimes feel more might have been done with me. I drink rather a lot."

"Oh," said Charles, because he felt called on to say something. The girl charmed him even though he heard in her candor an element of calculation; to which, indeed, she had admitted. Perhaps it was merely that he could not remember girls to have been so free-spoken in his youth, which all at once began to seem longer ago than it usually did.

"I was, you understand, not drunk, only gay," she continued. "I was happy for everyone because they were

26

all happy, but happiest for me because I was really, without strain, behaving like the most popular girl on campus and thinking how pleased Daddy would be that I hadn't been ruined by a European education but was perfectly willing and able to be ruined by an American one. It all looked harmless enough at the time, because Ray and I hardly seemed to be personally involved at all. We were public figures like the King and Queen of the May, and all the sheep in Alpha Sigma Sigma were gamboling around us building up sentiment, drinking toasts, warming themselves at the fire of romance.

"We were quite simply the best people there, the handsomest, the richest, the noblest—just the way it would be in a novel. I may not be much, but, dear me, I'm certainly aristocratic looking when dressed up, and said to be intelligent, and known to be rich; while Ray is dirt-poor, comes of the stock they use for building pyramids—this is not snobbism, or maybe it is, but I'm telling you how things seemed to a good many people at the time—and, finally, he was a hero and might make All-American. Only the brave deserve the fair.

"So when things dissolved a bit—when the boys, having shown their dates what a grand passion was, took them off into corners to what you might call reduce the myth to practical experience—Ray was tender, fumbling and romantic, and I, not to apologize for it, saw all this as perfectly splendid. He pinned his tiny pin just here over my heart, and he reverently did it, I may say, without trying to feel me up. Does this shock you or bore you?"

"I don't see quite where I come in," Charles said. "But go on if you like."

"I've never been much for doing things only because other people expected me to do them," the girl resumed, "and a week or so later, when I began to see that I was living in a dream which wasn't even my dream—nor quite, for that matter, Ray's dream, though he shared more of it than I did, but some kind of public dream about a poor boy of good character and a beautiful cold princess—why, I pinched myself and woke up.

"You can do that with your own dreams, pinch yourself and wake up, but to get out of somebody else's dream you've got to pinch somebody else. It wasn't till a week ago that I pinched Ray, and I haven't got round to pinching all the fraternity brothers, not to mention the rest of this college—for this romance got a certain publicity.

"I gave back the pin—last Monday night, I think. I was as gentle as possible about it—I said only that we ought not to engage ourselves even that far without being more certain than what a football season could make us; I didn't even, as yet, suggest our not seeing one another—but how gentle can one be, about a thing like that? It either is or it isn't. Ray was only bewildered at first, and beginning to be sort of sadly huffy. He finally said I had no right to do this to him—do you think that a fair statement?"

"It must have been a terrible disappointment," Charles said, wondering how one really did feel at that age, how he had felt under similar circumstances, and finding in his mind only the palest, most academic

28

imitation of what must have been, once, a flood of horror and loneliness at the remorseless revelation of oneself as someone not loved.

"By Tuesday night our hero had made up his mind," Lily Sayre continued, "and gave me to understand, on the phone it was, that unless I restored the status quo nothing was worth while to him, he was going to give up and 'quit everything.' I didn't understand then that what he meant was football. I had a little scary moment when the phone was silent and I thought he meant suicide or something, but then he started talking again and sounded like a clear case of moonshine and romantic sulks, so I thought to myself, 'well, he really is a simple young man, isn't he?' and I told him—I said —" Lily broke off and looked at Charles somewhat defiantly.

"Yes," Charles said, "you told him what?"

"It may have been the wrong thing to have said, or I said it the wrong way, but I told him to stop behaving like a poodle."

"That was tactful."

"I had to say something, didn't I? Maybe I should have waited till after the football season—but I couldn't have known, could I, that my decisions about my private life would cause odds to drop all over the nation?"

"You want me to understand that the boy deliberately failed my course and made himself ineligible," said Charles, "in order to teach you a lesson?"

"Just so," said Lily Sayre. "And by now a trifle worse than that. For he seems to have mentioned it to others;

29

at any rate there is a rumor going round to that effect, precisely. I have been seriously reproached for, if you please, want of school spirit, by Jane Parrot and Nancy Percy, both of them cheerleaders, and I expect to be visited shortly by the president of Alpha Sigma Sigma. If misery does indeed love company, you may cheer yourself by thinking that I'm under pressure too."

Charles laughed rather hopelessly.

"What do you suggest we do?" he asked.

"I'm still talking to you personally?" she said. "Talking to a man of sense? We are not talking about rules and how what's done is done?"

"Ah, as to that," he said, "I can't absolutely assure you."

"Then I don't suggest anything," Lily said, with neither coldness nor offense. "I must bear my cheap plastic cross as you must bear yours. I'm sorry." And she offered her hand.

"To gain your good opinion," Charles said, "I should call the boy in, give him a quick make-up exam, and pass him if he doesn't know one Cromwell from the other?"

"Yes," she said earnestly. "Exactly that. Get him out there, give him back his football—push it into his arms if necessary and tell him to run with it. Make him understand that no romantic nonsense is to be tolerated. He has a responsibility to his glorious career if not to his team and his college, and that responsibility is neither yours nor mine, but his. What I want of you may be immoral, I know that, but it is ethical—it's the only honest way, and if it's difficult for either of us, our hero is the one who ought to be punished for it . . . after tomorrow's game, though, if possible."

"And you?" Charles asked. "Do you take him back, likewise, till after tomorrow's game?"

She smiled at him more personally, as he thought, than before.

"You're shrewd, you see things," said she. "I like that."

Charles smiled back but remained silent, his question still in the air.

"I mustn't try to be seductive, right?" said Lily. "No, I won't take him back. I can't, only to chuck him out again afterward, can I? That would be unfair."

"You speak delightfully of 'us,' " Charles said glumly, "but of course you mean me. I doubt I can do what you ask, even though to an extent I agree with you—I'd have to hear the story from the boy himself, though, first. I'm sorry."

The noon bell began to strike.

"Don't take it to heart," said Lily Sayre. "I can realize that for a man, a teacher, the thing is more complicated. And I can see that you're right in asking me to play my part if you are to play yours—and I can't, I just can't."

"Where in all this is Blent?" Charles asked angrily. "Why does everyone come to tell me what a terrible thing I've done? Why doesn't he appear on the scene at all? I didn't flunk the damn exam. He did."

"You'll be late for your appointment," Lily said, picking up her coat.

"Listen," said Charles, "nothing is quite settled yet.

A good deal depends on this next hour. If I want you, where can I reach you?"

"I don't live at the college," she replied. "I live with my father in town, we're in the book."

They shook hands, and then, somewhat embarrassed, discovered that they were going out together anyhow. He helped her into her coat.

"Can I drive you anywhere?" Lily asked. "My father has provided me with a Bugatti. Every American girl ought to have one."

Charles, refusing this offer, saw her into the car.

"I'm sorry I'm not a man of sense," he said as she started the engine. "I hope you'll find one."

3

If there were indeed a situation, as there probably was, and if the revelation of Lily Sayre put that situation in a new light, as Charles thought on the whole it probably did not, officially speaking, he had just now at any rate no leisure to consider what his full response ought to be. He was a few moments late for his appointment with the President, and, while he did not ignominiously scurry, he did take the forbidden shortcut across the Oval to the administrative offices in Jackson Hall, with the result that he was frowned at by Miss Moriarty, Dean of Women, who stood on the top step enjoying a cigarette.

"Splendid morning, ma'am," Charles assured her as he plunged past.

"Indeed. I was just thinking," she replied, "how late the grass has remained green this year."

Charles prudently waited until the front door was between them before saying, in a pleasant voice, "I sincerely trust I have ruined your day."

The outside of Jackson Hall was traditionally ivy-covered, but the inside had been redone recently to make an impression consonant with the nature of administration: partitions had been knocked down and the entire area divided again not into rooms but into what architects call "space"—a maze of counters waist-high, within which barricades, and under very bright fluorescent lights, numerous secretaries worked at typewriters. The lights, set in batteries of what appeared to be large inverted ice-trays, reflected from clean, creamy walls, and the whole place radiated a sort of unquestioning and hygienic energy which made an agreeable effect even on Charles, who as a teacher had sometimes wondered what all these industrious ladies drew down their salaries for doing.

He stopped to announce his business to the switchboard operator, and only when she bade him wait did he begin to feel uncomfortable about what was to come. He should have had the last half-hour in which to anticipate and plan—"if he says this, then I say that," like a beginner at chess. But perhaps it was better this way, really; Charles felt himself to be the sort of person who improvises more skillfully than he composes, and briefly inspecting his attitude at this moment he was able, pleasingly, to find in it very little rigidity, stubbornness, or moral nonsense simply for the sake of moral nonsense. His position, though it would have been better without those two undergraduate ward

33

heelers, remained a reasonable one and he should present it reasonably. Thus far he had got when the switchboard lady waved him onward.

Nevertheless he felt, as always, an irrational uneasiness at entering the offices of the President of the College, at penetrating to the *oeil de boeuf, les appartements de son altesse.* It was not, indeed, a personal feeling, for he got on quite well with Harmon Nagel, but rather a sense of the mystery of authority, such a sense as everyone gets on being summoned to the principal's office for the first time, and as some people never lose thereafter. Perhaps the essence of it all, too, which came to him always as a discovery of something new, was the fact that here at the top, or in the center, of things, after climbing the hierarchy of all that was official, impersonal, delegated, or even, you might say, subinfeudated—the dingy offices full of schoolroom furniture and old textbooks—you arrived back finally at the richly personal, the clean, delightful room full of a cheerfully reflected daylight, the small fire behind the bright brass knobs of the andirons, the plain but good carpeting, the long, shining, polished desk. On the walls hung pictures of the President's own choice, no doubt, and the bookcases were stocked with books which, some of them still in their bright dust-jackets, had the confident, informal air of being there because the President wanted them to be there.

Even as Miss Yarrow held open the door for Charles while announcing his entrance, Dr. Nagel was on his feet and coming around the corner of the desk to shake hands.

34

"Charles," he said in so warm a way as to leave no doubt of his genuine pleasure.

"Sir, it's nice to see you," said Charles. He might have said "Harmon," he might without giving offense have merely said "Hi," but felt that for the moment the respect and reserve equally implied by "sir" defined things better. There were many ways of using that form of address; he hoped his own approximated that of Dr. Johnson in a mild mood: the dignified acknowledgment of authority, rejection of familiarity, the courteous but firm suggestion that all forms of life had an equal right to existence. Nagel, on his side, was clearly sensitive to this shading; he frowned just a trifle; and clearly, also, sensitive enough to make no point of it. He indicated to Charles a chair beside the desk, and himself resumed his own place behind it, where he sat for a long moment in silence, hands behind his head, regarding Charles with a serious yet friendly smile, which Charles returned.

"You may have troubles," Harmon Nagel said presently, "but at least you're not a college president. You know that common belief of the Middle Ages—that a bishop, simply for being a bishop, couldn't escape being damned as a matter of course? That's what it is to be president of a college."

Charles made a small sympathetic noise.

"A medium-sized, liberal arts college," the President continued, "of Baptist origins and Republican sympathies, charmingly located in rural surroundings near the prosperous town of ———; at least they were rural, but there's a kind of college slum of laundries, bars and lunch-counters, moving in on us at the foot of the hill. Charles, is it true, would you know, that Mike's College Café is in fact only the front parlor of, to speak plainly, a whorehouse?"

"I've heard it mentioned," said Charles.

"Yes. Why, oh why are these children incapable of keeping quiet about their wicked pleasures? Now something will have to be done about that. And look at this." He lifted a number of documents in a pile off his desk and let them fall hopelessly back.

"For example—Mrs. Parrish, whose late husband was a trustee of this institution until, I think, 1937, wonders why the College has stopped sending her football tickets. She wonders in a very firm way, and as Mrs. Parrish has a good deal of money which she may leave to us, the issue is a reckonable one. For example— the Pittsburgh alumni group, having evidently discovered after all these years what *something* is about, sends a document calling upon the College to reject the traditions of pagan Greece and put its education on the unshakable basis, as they call it, of the Christian faith; they are full of practical suggestions, which I must answer somehow, as to how we may accomplish this desirable reform, and end by asking me flatly how I can defend 'the arrogant secular philosophies of Athens and Rome.' "

"You might ask them to work out their scheme in full detail," Charles said. "That would give you a few years, during which they'd probably forget the whole thing."

"Ah, Charles, watch out. I see you've an element of

administrative stuff in you. One last example—the captain of the State Troopers barracked out on route 10 is holding in custody one of our young gentlemen who last Monday night parked his car largely in, I gather, the space occupied by a patrol car. Upon being reprimanded, our young scholar, who was also drunk, had words with the officer, who felt compelled to arrest him; whereon it gradually becomes clear that the boy has borrowed the car from a classmate for the evening, that the car is not insured, and that the driver is not the possessor of an operator's license. *Nevertheless*, Captain Price assures me—nevertheless, he hates to make trouble for the College, toward which he has always had the friendliest feelings. Nevertheless—*but*. The student's parents, who had been informed, telephoned this morning to say that I must certainly be mistaken about *all* the facts in the case, because their little boy would never do anything of that sort, and besides, they were quite sure he had never learned to drive. So there, with me in the middle, the matter uneasily rests.

"Charles, you think I'm trying to soften you up with tales of woe, don't you?" The President laughed, a happy, youthful laugh. "I am, too. It's such a pleasure to be able to say such things to someone now and then. Not with any dreadful motive, though," he added earnestly. "I do want sympathy once in a while, as anyone does. But please, Charles, don't sit there looking so grim, as though I were about to demand the sacrifice of your honor."

"Well, after all," said Charles, though with a smile, "aren't you?"

"Certainly not," Nagel replied at once, adding after a moment, "Don't think I wouldn't, though, if it seemed necessary."

Charles nodded his acceptance of this statement, which, because he believed it to be quite true, had a somewhat relaxing effect on him.

"Look here, Charles," the President went on, "I like you and I respect you, I think you're a fine teacher, and I know that like most fine teachers you operate on the basis of a quiet contempt for administration and the people who do it. I can quite easily imagine your judgment of myself, for example—'Nagel? Oh, a very nice fellow, but, of course, ruined by his job. He might have been a teacher, but he became a streamlined desk-set.' You'd say this, Charles, in a decent voice, that is, without pity or scorn but simply allowing it to appear that the situation is thus and not other than thus."

Charles wanted to put in a word here, modifying this impression, but Nagel waved him back.

"I neither resent your feeling that way nor blame you for it," he said. "I'd go further and say that in a sense you are right. I used to be a teacher, as you know, and felt the same way myself, once. Now sometimes I look in the mirror at my keen, intellectual, gray face, and I say, 'You're a distinguished educator now, kid.'" He laughed. "When I was a boy, an 'educator' was a kind of biscuit. It might better have stayed that way."

"Somebody has to run things," Charles said feebly.

"As much as to say, 'there must be janitors.' But it's true, nonetheless, and I am the somebody who runs things at this College. I wonder if you've thought much,

38

Charles, about what that means and what it's likely to cost—running things? I never did until I took this job; it's something teachers don't often take into account, as after all why should they?

"On my night-table," he continued, "there is a copy of the Holy Bible, and on top of that is a copy of *The Prince*. I find both books almost equally useful, but *The Prince* is on top.

"With certain reservations—we don't often deal literally in matters of life and death here, and perhaps that's why we have academic freedom, the freedom, that is, to be academic—but with few reservations, after all, a college president is in much the same situation as the prince Machiavelli described. He may rise to his eminence, for example, in a number of ways, some of them extraordinarily like usurpation or conquest. He rules 'his people,' that is, the students, and in direct contact with them he is kind, condescending in the best sense, genial, and full of authority, so full that he seems far above the need to use it—in direct contact, that is. At the same time, he is a little remote and inaccessible and mysterious because he is not merely authority, he is the principle of authority embodied and made visible.

"But it is the nobility—his faculty—and the courtiers —his administration—from whom he has most to gain and most to fear. The great robber barons of Sociology, English, the Physical Sciences . . . you follow me? He rules these, but only as *primus inter pares;* that's as far as the book takes him. The rest depends upon himself, what he lets them make of him personally. And they are smart men, Charles; one way and another, even the

39

dreamiest fuddy-duddy who sits in the library eating and eating from the *Domesday Book* or the *Principia*, even he is a smart man, and a college president could be knocked off his eminence by such a man and never even be able to imagine how or why.

"Then, beyond all that, there are alumni and trustees, and beyond them, the world, other princedoms, other hierarchies, authorities, deities, compared with which this eminence becomes invisibly small—and yet the prince must keep his balance, and if possible even his dignity, among all those forces."

"We've all got upper and nether millstones," said Charles, "if that's what you're trying to tell me. And if you mean that my failing Blent has put you under pressure, well, I'm sorry."

"Oh, that," said Nagel, dismissing 'that' with a scornful push of the hand. "Pressure. I'll bear up under my pressures, thanks. There are some, but they needn't have anything to do with you. And I want to say this, Charles—you were perfectly within your competence in flunking the boy if he wrote a bad exam. If anyone comes to brace you about it, you didn't make the student ineligible, the College itself did that."

Charles said mildly, "Did you call me in to offer congratulations?"

"You teachers are a defensive lot," the President said. "Of course I'm sorry Blent can't play. I stand to lose ten dollars to Dr. Parnell, our opponents' president—if Blent is as important as he's said to be, which I incline to doubt. But no—in principle, Charles, I'm with you all the way. I don't in the least mind seeing these football people put in their places once in a while."

"That was not the principle involved," Charles said.

"It can't help being," said Nagel, and swiveled around away from Charles to look out the window.

"It's perfectly true," he began a moment later, "that I asked you in to see if there were any chance of your changing your mind. In my position, as I've generally outlined it to you, and you needn't have details unless you want them, I couldn't do otherwise. I said I'd see you. But mark this, my friend. I am going to ask you if you can change this decision—but that's all. If, after I've put the position to you, you say you cannot do so, that is all, the last word. You needn't fear reprisals—not that you would—from this office or elsewhere; and I will support your decision, and the whole business will blow over."

"Thank you," said Charles a little self-consciously.

"Well, then." The President swiveled back to the desk and picked up a thick Manila folder, which he weighed on his hand for a moment.

"Doesn't it strike you as a trifle odd," he asked, "that this boy should up and fail an Hour Exam?"

"He failed it about as badly as he could," Charles replied. "He's never been in a class of mine before, so this is the first work of his I've seen, but I'm told he is supposed to be a pretty bright boy as well as everything else."

"Yes. You know, he didn't even come here on an athletic scholarship—we do give them, as you doubtless know. He has a scholarship, but he got it the hard way, that is, in the routine manner. Well, he had a little trouble right at the beginning of his career. He very nearly flunked out, and probably he would have done— I grant you this—if the freshman coach had not by that time discovered his talent and got Coach Hardy to intercede. This intercession was not based directly on football—naturally. It became a matter of *psychology,* if you please—you can't imagine how all that jargon about repressions and blocks has invaded the locker room these days—and Hardy managed to convince Dean Loring that Blent could be saved, academically and personally, by a bit of psychiatric guidance. So Blent was taken along to Dr. Blumenthal and given whatever it is that school psychiatrists give; nothing so deep, I'm sure, but it worked."

Dr. Nagel flapped the Manila folder, which he continued to hold.

"There are some confidential remarks in here," he said, "about shyness and insecurity and all that, and the results of tests which are confidential largely because I've no idea what they all mean. But at any rate the boy recovered and became not merely a passing student but a rather good one. And now here he is again, three years later—what does that add up to?"

"Not much," said Charles. "Take him to Blumenthal again. If the boy passes the mid-year exam he doesn't flunk the course."

"But meanwhile he is ineligible to play football?"

"That's the way it looks."

"Well, Charles, I can understand the line you're taking. It seems a little ruthless, not on our account so much as on Blent's—these boys, some of them, you know, can make a living at football when they leave here—but academically, and otherwise too for that matter, I'm not against ruthlessness as a matter of principle."

Dr. Nagel swung himself upright in his chair and got on his feet.

"I've had my say." He held out his hand. "I said, and you replied. Don't think evil thoughts, Charles. I do understand."

"I doubt you do," Charles said. "I doubt anybody does, and it's got me annoyed. You say you don't want to put pressure on me, and I believe you, or at any rate I believe you mean it. But personal pressure is a bit harder than the other, institutional kind. In effect you are saying to me that we two are so intelligent, so humane, so full of wisdom, and capable of seeing so far beyond the rules, that we can agree to give the boy a chance. And I'm in accord with that view, really—it's a charming way of doing things. And under the proper circumstances I'd do it that way."

"Go on," the President said, sitting down again.

"The proper circumstances—and I've done things that way on numerous occasions, and not necessarily having to do with football players, but with any student. I don't live by the rules altogether, and I certainly don't live for the rules. But why wouldn't the boy come to me himself? Why is it left to seven sorts of administration to ask me in various tones of voice whether I won't be a little less of a monster than usual, just this once? I am not a monster."

"You've had some trouble over this already?"

"A little," Charles said, and briefly outlined his interview with the representatives of the student government. He did not think it necessary to mention Lily Sayre.

"So now you feel it's made a matter of principle and taken out of your hands?"

"Even that wouldn't bother me," Charles said. "I can live without the good opinion of the local leaders. My point is that the situation is a personal one, or was, and the student should have had sense enough to know it. How do I know what Blent thinks or wants?" he cried a bit wildly. "Maybe he has perfectly good reasons for wanting to stay out of football, maybe he wants to flunk out of school—how do you know he wants all these efforts made on his behalf?"

"I'd be perfectly willing to have a word with Barber and Da Silva," said Nagel, "if you felt that would leave you free to make your own decision."

"I don't need police protection, yet," Charles replied. "And as for my decision, I thought I'd made it.

"Look here," he continued more mildly, "I don't want to stand on principles. I never do. Principles are too narrow to stand on, and everybody teeters ridiculously. I quite agree with what you imply and don't say —that the entire business is a puerile one, and not worth getting so involved with. Put it this way. I'll be in my office this afternoon from two until four. If Blent shows up, I'll talk with him. But I don't intend to send him an invitation, and I don't promise anything will come of it. If he comes to me, and if he can offer any sort of convincing reason for having done badly, and any prospect of doing better—which is unlikely, as why should he be prepared any better than he was when he took the test?—I'm willing to give him a chance. Is that fair?"

"Meaning that it's my business to see that the boy gets there?"

"If you want him to get there—yes."

"Not only fair, Charles, it's generous." The President stood up again, and they shook hands. "By the way," he added, "Mrs. Nagel and I are having a little cocktail affair for some of the alumni and the trustees and a few of the faculty. Five o'clock. I hope you'll join us then."

"And deliver my official report?" asked Charles, who had to return Dr. Nagel's pleasant smile because it seemed to him to represent the mere impudence, rather than the arrogance, of power.

"We'd take it as a favor if you would come," Dr. Nagel gravely assured him.

"Don't get all hopeful," Charles said as he left. "I've not promised you anything. Your ten dollars is not safe yet."

2

Football produced in Charles Osman some subtle tensions which he had never bothered to inspect very closely, which in fact he had constantly kept away from reflection out of a feeling that some parts of one's own history were better left unexamined so long as they themselves set up no clamor. These tensions nevertheless kept him interested in the game enough that he habitually went to see it played on Saturdays and even felt a trifle lost when the College team played away; despite that, as he perfectly knew, the strange and difficult feelings aroused in him and brought to a pitch of some urgency by the game itself always issued in a deep melancholy that colored Saturday night and lasted well over into the Sunday; so much so that by now even his nervous enthusiasms of Friday afternoon bore the melancholy of anticipation. His double sense of excitement and oppression of spirit was strong enough for him to have sometimes resolved to "break himself of the habit" of watching such contests; but he had not yet been successful in this moral enterprise.

Indeed, there was some reason for tension; by Friday afternoon in the season a kind of generalized pressure began to build up on the campus, such a pressure as one might expect to feel in a city about to declare war: a hastening, a conspiratorial huddling in the street, the appearance of strange faces, a sudden plenty of strange automobiles (on Homecoming Weekend one saw so many black Cadillacs) from which emerged grave, elderly, statesmanlike persons who looked about them with some sort of decisive assurance and drew one or two deep breaths before entering their old fraternity house. This pressure had to do with football, yes, but was no less real for all that, and had to be felt even by persons who did not care for the game and believed it to be, in fact, stupid; there was no denying that *something* could be felt gathering force. And this anticipatory stir and bustle, not altogether pleasant, perhaps a trifle ominous, got an accent from the fact that somewhere in the distance the band was practicing—far enough in the distance, around enough stone corners, that one hardly heard the music but received instead, through the stomach rather than the ears, a deep beating of some common heart, as though the air itself had just perceptibly grown rhythmical, with such momentary loud intimations of music as might be heard several streets away from a parade, making a man straighten his shoulders and stride out even if he has no intention of going to the parade.

Charles would go to the parade, but he resented any straightening of shoulders to match, any implication of his being forced to march in step to the music, so on Friday afternoons during the fall he retired to his office at the back of the third-floor stack of the library and settled down there with a detective story. It was a very peaceful place in that corner of time, which he had made peculiarly his own; from a bottle of whisky kept in the desk drawer he took occasional sips, not much but enough to make some sort of golden inward glow that matched the cold golden glow of the sun outside. This habit represented for Charles the slight insolence, the trivial liberty, which it was nearly a point of honor with him to take in any position, and without which no position would be worth holding; therefore he resented the probable appearance, sometime during the afternoon, of Raymond Blent, which had the effect of pinning him to this place even if it would have been the place of his free choice.

He had had lunch downtown at a restaurant traditionally associated with the College, the Aaron Burr, and found the dining room disagreeably full—as he might have anticipated—of alumni. Mr. Giardineri, the owner, whom Charles admired perhaps unreasonably because he had not changed his name to Gardiner upon the purchase of so historic a property, had come over to his table to pass one or two remarks of a friendly sort, based not on friendship but on the sense of their community as residents among all these transients.

"I hate this weekend," Giardineri had observed.

"You do a good business, though," Charles replied.

"Take the business and leave me in peace. Every year we play at home these babies wreck the place. I'm two weeks cleaning up after them. They want to be boys and girls again."

"Maybe we'll lose," said Charles. "Then they'll only sit and weep and all you'll have to worry about will be flood damage."

"If we win, we do the damage, if they win, they do the damage—what's the difference? A funny thing, though," Mr. Giardineri added, "if we lose there's about fifty bucks less damage when I get the place fixed up. The visitors are always polite; they don't remember to break the windows before they go home. Say, by the way, Professor," he went on, reminded of something.

"Don't call me Professor," Charles said.

"I hear the faculty's fixed it so we lose tomorrow."

"It gets around, doesn't it?"

"You hear a lot in a place like this, if you listen to it." The proprietor stooped a little closer and spoke confidentially.

"It don't make any difference Blent not playing," he said. "The smart money's been on the other boys for two weeks. I know you're not the kind of guy who would bet against his own outfit, Professor, but I'm just telling you in case you put any money on us—we're out, they're in."

"You're absolutely certain of that?" Charles said. "Are they going to bother playing the game, or do the losers pay up now?"

"I'm not kidding," Giardineri said with great earnestness. "There's professional money gone into this, from New York. Somebody's making a big book, and I think I know who the guys are."

"Mr. Giardineri, you surprise and shock me," said Charles, "by implying that our fine young athletes are controlled by a Syndicate from the Big City."

"You're kidding me, Professor," said Giardineri. "But just remember what I'm telling you—the other boys win, and the point spread is twelve points."

"Let me surprise and shock you," Charles said. "Blent might play after all—he might."

"Makes no difference."

"Mr. Giardineri, since you're so almighty positive, I'll do this for you—if Blent plays, I'll show my loyalty to Alma Mater by giving you five dollars even."

"Mr. Osman, you professors can't afford to do that—I read about your salaries every week in the papers and my heart bleeds."

"Nevertheless," Charles said firmly, and it was done.

A silly thing to do, Charles now thought in the privacy of his office. The money did not matter—he had been only partly serious in offering a bet, but annoyed at the other man's air of smug certainty. What mattered was his having involved himself directly, even if trivially, in the affair Blent, so that he might afterward appear to have stood to gain (as people would say reprovingly) by allowing the boy to play.

As to that, the question of Blent's playing or not playing stood squarely up to Charles. He had left the President's office feeling on the whole pleased with himself and President Nagel. They had both shown themselves tolerant, mature, and wise. He himself had demonstrated the utmost reasonableness in order to show that he was "not a monster," but at the same time he had promised nothing against his conscience.

By the time he had finished lunch this view of the matter seemed unsatisfactory, and as he sat at his desk sipping whisky from a paper cup and reading a dreadful mystery in flagrant contempt of the army of unalterable law drawn up in shelves above, below and around him, Charles began to feel that he had given his little finger to the devil, and that the hand, arm, and whole person must follow.

Clearly he need not see Blent simply in order to reiterate that things were as they were; in promising to speak to the student at all he had implied the next step, that things would be changed by that interview. And as he had blandly announced to the President, there was no reason to suppose that Blent had occupied himself since being declared ineligible in the study of English History; therefore he would no doubt flunk any make-up exam given at this time. Therefore, it was clear, he, Charles Osman, was invited to do exactly what he had proclaimed he would not and could not do, that is, in young Mr. da Silva's deliciously loathsome phrase, "flannel things over."

Clearest of all, and worst, Charles had positively invited himself into the situation. President Nagel—who suddenly looked less tolerant but much wiser than he had before—had allowed him to do, of his own free will, on his own initiative, exactly what President Nagel must probably have desired of him; by withholding the expected pressure he had enabled Charles to fall on his own face with an air of triumphant and humane rationality which must have looked extremely funny, at least to President Nagel.

"No, I am not a monster," he said aloud. "But I'm not so bright, either." And he imagined in some disgust his appearance at the President's cocktail party—he could scarcely either fail to show up, or show up merely to announce that Blent was still ineligible—to deliver, as he had put it so blithely, his official report. Like any ward heeler, any political henchman.

"I might, though," he said grimly—meaning that he might, despite everything, hew to his own line. "I might surprise hell out of everyone."

What annoyed him perhaps most of all at this moment was his so largely proclaimed wish to see Blent personally, face to face. What had he meant, what had he imagined might be accomplished, by that? Oh, on the surface it was no doubt justifiable and better than that—it was tolerant, humane Mr. Chips putting personal relations above principles. Inspected more closely, did it reflect in Charles any deeper wish to be acquainted with Raymond Blent? Charles, who was disagreeably sensitive to remote resonances in the mind, felt the fleeting pathos of those early years during which he himself had wanted to be a football star, when he had stood before the mirror at home, dressed in football uniform with a ball under his arm, and practiced those prancing postures and snarling expressions conventionally used in photographs and cartoons of his heroes. This pathetic and grotesque apparition from childhood depressed him; he remembered how ashamed he had been when his sister suddenly opened the door one day and caught him grimacing there, standing on one leg, running fiercely, without motion, into the silence of the mirror.

He had wanted to be a star on the world's great stage, but became instead a teacher of history. In high school, later on, he had been a second-string fullback—"tailback," "bucking-back," with what impudence those phrases now proclaimed their sad and vanished glory! —while at college he had not even tried out for the team (which he would have had no hope of making in any case).

In college he had belonged to that section of the intelligentsia which despised football and all who played it, but which went to the games nevertheless; the fine distinction of the attitude being enforced on the moral side by the test of one's ability to sit in the cheering section (to which one was assigned) without cheering. It was from this period of his life chiefly that Charles remembered his tensions about football to have begun: the nervous elation of Saturdays, the hollowness in the stomach as severe as though he himself were going to play—

sometimes he could not bear to eat his lunch—the cold splendor of the afternoon and the great resonance of sounds in the stadium . . . and then the intense disappointment, win or lose, when the shadows grew over the field, the air got colder, and the clock ran out. And the melancholy of Sundays, when the football game, which had stood like a solid bulwark in time, had fallen like all else, allowing that remorseless flood to sweep onward toward Monday and the week's work. It had been the first major hint, perhaps, for Charles, or at any rate the first hint consciously taken, of the disastrous impermanence of all things, of death which awaited both failure and success; the image, even, of the crumbling of dynasties and empires. Perhaps, even, this half-realization of the fluidity of all that seemed most solid, of one's grasp on life as fundamentally condemned to disappointment, had not merely reflected but in part determined his wish to study history; as though by that means one saved a few precious, meaningless, damaged objects from the generally ruining flood.

To meditate thus was all very well, and even soothing to the spirit. Yet it remained that there was now nothing to do but wait for Blent's appearance, assuming meanwhile, like an Old Testament prophet, that the Lord would put words in one's mouth. Charles took a sip of whisky and forced himself to attend to his mystery story; but at once, to his intensified and troubled consciousness, the first words he read took on an intimately personal sense—it was as though any book, at such a time, might become a message to oneself, from which, however dubiously, sibylline sortileges were to be drawn.

The detective—who, be it noted, was sitting at his desk and drinking whisky from a bottle kept in the drawer—spoke thus on his method, to a rich girl in a mink coat:

"*I lie to people,*" he said. "*I find that if you lie to people enough, they get confused, until finally one of them tells you the truth by accident.*"

It was a deep sentence, thought Charles—oracular, ambiguous, capable of the utmost expansions; surely that was what everyone did?

Steps echoed uncertainly, with pauses, on the flooring outside; a shadow appeared on the glass door; there came a tentative knocking.

"Come in," Charles said, resisting a conscious impulse to hide the whisky and the detective story; he absolutely refused to allow himself to be ashamed before a student. After all, he thought, you are a grownup now.

It was not Blent, however, but Coach Hardy (Charles could not recall offhand his first name). The coach was a small, lively-looking man, bald, with a freckled scalp, light mustache, light hairs growing in tufts in his ears, and very pale eyes. He wore a chesterfield somewhat frayed as to its velvet, and carried a black Homburg; but beneath the coat as he threw it open he had on sweat shirt and baseball pants—as though, Charles thought, he had been caught midway in the transformation from weekday character-builder to the supreme *strategos* of Saturday afternoon.

"How do, Coach," he said politely, nodding to the other chair.

"You're not an easy man to find, Dr. Osman," said the coach as he sat down.

Charles frowned at this implication that he had somehow been hiding from the consequences of his actions.

"I mean," the coach added on seeing this expression, "I mean this is a mighty complicated building—I don't get in here much, and for a while I thought I was going to have to stay here all night."

"They did find the skeleton of a student in here once," Charles said quite seriously; the coach smiled, but not with absolute certainty. "Poor fellow evidently starved."

"Ah." The coach smiled a trifle more broadly, but still testing. "I'm afraid we haven't met," he said, "but I've seen you at faculty meetings. They make me go to faculty meetings, you know," he added in a kind of sad apology.

"It's all education," Charles said, "I guess."

This offer seemed to reassure the coach; he lifted his head slightly, and the pale eyes twinkled, Charles thought, rather professionally. His own coach in high school had been able to twinkle like that; it was quite a trick.

"I'm glad you see it that way, Dr. Osman," Hardy said. "It's always been my line—we work together, you in the classroom and us out on the field. *Mens sana in corpore sano,*" he enunciated, not easily.

"What?" Charles asked.

"*Mens sana in corpore sano,*" said Coach Hardy. "A sound mind in a sound body," he explained uncomfortably.

"Oh," said Charles. "Well, I'm glad to hear it."

There was a silence after this exchange.

"I just came round to say," the coach finally began, "that I really appreciate, we all appreciate, over at the field house, what you're doing for us. Dr. Nagel phoned me to say we had you to thank."

"I haven't done it yet," Charles pointed out. The coach smiled a smile of somewhat queasy complicity, then frowned and looked down at his hat.

"We're having a last, light workout," he said. "Just signal drill. But I told Ray to crack those books for a couple of hours. He's with the tutor now, and I'll have him here for you at four, don't worry about that, Dr. Osman." He smiled again. "Ray is a good boy, fundamentally," he said. "He won't let us down."

"Would you like some whisky?" Charles asked.

"Oh, no thanks, sir. I've got this stomach condition. You go ahead, though."

"Well, then, Coach, what can I do for you?"

"Now, I didn't come round to beg favors, Dr. Osman," said Hardy, raising a hand as in warning against the thought. "I just thought sometimes it's nice to show you appreciate a man's putting himself out for you. I just wanted to say thanks."

"Tell me something," said Charles. "Is Blent so important? Can any one man be so important?"

"Ah, that's hard to say. Football is a team game, Dr. Osman. It's not the eighty-yard run that everybody sees —that's not the only thing. Sometimes, if it weren't for a tackle or guard who's in there doing the work even if he never gets in the papers . . ."

"I mean without the lecture. Is Blent that important?"

"He's pretty important," said the coach. "In a small school like this, you don't have much depth—"

"I've found that to be true, too."

"You don't have much depth, and especially not in a key position where you need brains. Ray is a fine field-general; that means more to me, to us—his directing the team on offense—than his running and passing, even. Back of him, I tell you in confidence, Dr. Osman, we got, well, pretty average material—stumble-bums, you might say, prelim boys, claimers. I've been praying all season nothing would happen to the boy—that he wouldn't get hurt. And now this happens to his studies. That I never expected."

"And one football game—is that important?"

The coach looked keenly at Charles, who now caught a glimpse of something other than the fumbling, imprecise leader of Boy Scouts in this man's character; something a good deal colder and harder.

"We've had an undefeated season," he pointed out. "This school hasn't had the chance of an undefeated season for twelve years. The other boys are good, too, and they've been beat once. They'll be laying for us hard."

"So you could lose a game," Charles insisted. "Do you care so much?"

"It's what I'm in it for, to care that much." The coach leaned forward confidentially and said, "I developed Blent. When he looks good, I look good. I'll be honest with you, Dr. Osman. You professors live a kind of protected life—sure, you don't get much dough, but in return for that you get a lot of pressures taken off you, you don't have to compete. I have to compete."

"So?"

"So—and I'm telling you this because I know you're a good head, Doctor—I could still be on the way up in my business. An undefeated year, good statistics, lots of space in the papers, and I could be on my way. I could write my own ticket somewhere big, Michigan State, Oklahoma, maybe—that kind of thing. And I'll tell you this: I've thought of taking Ray along, backfield coach, unless he wants to play pro ball, which he could do."

"This place is only a rung on the ladder, eh?"

"Don't get me wrong, Dr. Osman. I like this school fine. I think it's a first-rate institution of learning, sir."

"Only it's sort of tenth-rate?" put in Charles, and the coach looked at him most carefully before replying.

"That's it," he said earnestly. "In my line of work it's crummy. Blent was a big break—if he'd played in high school he'd have been snapped up by some major outfit before we ever saw him. Of course," he added modestly, "I helped develop the boy, and it's no joke starting from scratch even if a kid has talent.

"I like Ray," he said with finality, "and I'd like to see him win. That's why I'm here."

"And he can't win unless he can play," Charles said with a smile.

"Now, sir, don't get the idea I'm trying to put pressure on you—"

"Do you know," said Charles, "you're the fifth person who hasn't been trying to put pressure on me today? I feel as if I were in a vacuum."

The coach, moving steadily downfield now, disregarded this irrelevance.

"I realize you've got your standards, Dr. Osman," he said, "and I'm not asking you to fake one damn thing. I only ask this—don't get the boy personally upset, you know what I mean? Ray is a very nervous and insecure kid in some ways, tends to go back into himself in trouble, and brood. I happen to know he had a very sad childhood, the family situation was not good, the parents separated many years ago—the boy is brilliant, I can tell you that for sure, you must have seen it yourself, but he's not happy. That Blumenthal, that doctor we had him to three years ago, told me some shocking things . . ."

"Meaning?"

"The boy tried to knock himself off once, when he was a freshman—did you know that?"

"Great field generals sometimes do come sort of queer," said Charles, rubbing his chin. "Charles XII, Napoleon, Nelson . . . But dear me—you sound as if the boy ought to be in bed under competent care."

"Oh, now, nothing like that, nothing like that. Ray is perfectly sound; all that's in the past, long over and done with. I only don't want him to get upset in any way the night before the game."

"Meaning you might decide to run him even if he stays ineligible?" asked Charles.

"Professor Osman," said the coach, fixing him with a firm and honest glance, "you know that would be impossible." A small flicker of connivance crossed the honest glance and was gone.

"Well." Charles thought for a long moment. His position, which he had so admired all morning, seemed to have become untenable.

"I'll talk with the boy," he said, "and I can't promise you anything but this, that I'm not going to go out of my way to make it difficult for him. Fair enough?"

The coach's ready smile and firm handclasp as he got up seemed to Charles a ritual gesture sealing him securely among the confraternity of the morally dubious; his firm principles, taken together with his broad and understanding humanity, had in a few hours made him a shady character.

"You're a good man, sir," said Coach Hardy. "Now if we can get the other guy to co-operate, we're all set."

"*Other guy?*"

"This damn radical in the philosophy department, this Solomon creep." The coach's sandy eyebrows raised themselves in amazement. "You didn't know? Nobody told you? Yeah, Ray flunked his course too." He straightened himself up to leave. "That can be taken care of, though," he assured Charles, who simply stood there with his mouth open.

"I hope you're coming to the game, sir," Coach Hardy said as he went. "If you haven't got a ticket, phone the student manager at the field house and tell him I said to give you a good seat."

2

If Charles, earlier in the day, had wanted a view of certain realities, he now began to have it; if he had been exhilarated by the dramatic sense of "a situation," this sort of exhilaration now amply opened its possibility before him, for there could be no doubt, upon Coach Hardy's clearly accidental disclosure, of his being at this moment in a situation. He felt, as a matter of fact, angry, depressed, and confused, and for a few minutes could do nothing but walk rapidly up and down the cramped space of his office like a man in a cage—a furnished cage, however, in which he kept stumbling over one or the other chair. Catching sight of that detective story on his desk, he snatched it up and read again that mysterious sentence: *"I find that if you lie to people enough, they get confused, until finally one of them tells you the truth by accident."*

"How true, O Private Eye," said Charles, continuing to pace.

So all those people—the wise and the stupid alike, the generous and the mean—had carefully avoided giving him the whole truth of his situation. They had allowed him to assume that the decision was his, and that, knowing all the circumstances, he could be secure of its consequences. Clearly those students must have known, Barber and Da Silva, since they had held a meeting on the subject the night before. President Nagel must have known. Lily Sayre need not have known—he liked to think she did not—but of course she might have. As for the coach, he had simply assumed Charles must know; which was, indeed, a sufficient excuse for the others if they cared to make use of it: Blent's failure in the other course, as in his own, was a public matter of record; there was no particular reason for Charles either to know it or be ignorant of it. He had merely assumed—

but it appeared that others had assumed he would so assume, and that they had had, as Hardy's exclamation showed—"You didn't know? Nobody told you?"— not the slightest intention of correcting his assumption.

The acceptance and understanding of this radical change in the affair was as difficult for Charles, during these few minutes, as the move from a Ptolemaic to a Copernican universe—or so he put it, seeing himself as suddenly removed from his sound and simple relation to the center of things and forced to substitute all at once a more multiplied, problematic view of all sorts of attractions and repulsions.

The other man, Solomon—had he been treated in the same way, allowed to believe that he bore all the responsibility alone, and that, as a corollary, the decision also belonged to him alone? And had he, as the coach implied, refused to give in, either out of stubbornness and dislike of athletes ("this Solomon creep") or for some deeper reason ("this damn radical in the philosophy department")?

Or—what was both much worse and more likely—had the principle of divide and conquer been differently employed? That is, had someone, or everyone, decided to go to work on Charles first, since he was the easier of the two, and then use his agreement as a lever with which to move Mr. Solomon? If that were indeed the way of it, then the force exerted on Solomon must have mightily increased since Charles's interview with President Nagel.

"Come, Solomon, your colleague has been a good sport about this thing, give us a break."

"Solomon, there's no point in standing alone against the world."

"Why not be reasonable, Mr. Solomon? Charles Osman was reasonable."

Charles was horrified at having thus, though unawares, betrayed a colleague. His actions, seen in this new light, not merely failed of being good union behavior; they positively took him over to the other side; he was a scab. All was made worse by the consideration that, though he did not know Mr. Solomon at all well, he did not much like what he knew; and therein, in the matter of Mr. Solomon's character, personality, career, and very being, lay some ethical tensions which Charles would much have preferred not to have to contemplate just at this moment.

Nonetheless, this contemplation had now become necessary, since in the half-hour or so remaining before Blent was to show up, Charles must come to his decision all over again, and this decision involved himself more intimately than had ever appeared possible until now.

The two of them, Charles Osman and Solomon—Leon was his first name—were in many ways opposites, which meant that they had a great deal in common. One could say, Charles thought, that they were *intimately opposed*. Worlds apart at first glance, a closer inspection suggested to him that they were like distorted images of one another, in a comparison which could work to the advantage of neither; they were *mirror-opposites*.

They were just about of an age, but Solomon was a failure, one of those persons who for various reasons move from college to college without ever getting anywhere, a kind of academic tramp. Here in his late thirties, married, with children—two, was it, or three?— he remained an instructor despite his very considerable experience, learning, and acknowledged intelligence; whereas Charles had been an associate professor for two years and would naturally in the course of events rise to his full professorship and probably, if he stayed on here, would become head of the History Department on Lestrange's retirement, say in ten years.

Charles had to smile, even in his present mood, at the view of himself as a *success:* truly, in the academic world, small satisfactions went a long way. But the point was that he could afford to smile where Solomon could at best afford to sneer. And in the academic world no less than in others, failure was felt to have its contagious quality—could it have been on this account that Charles never went out of his way to become acquainted with Leon Solomon?

To be perfectly strict about it, since he was being perfectly strict, Charles did not have to reproach himself on this account. The College was not a huge one, but large enough nevertheless so that one did not have to know everybody. He and Solomon were not even in the same department, though affiliated even so in that nebulous mass called the Social Sciences; there was little enough to bring them together in the ordinary course of days and semesters.

But Solomon was Jewish. Charles was Jewish. The College around them, while no doubt perfectly secular except for ceremonial acknowledgments, was neverthe- less Christian in its foundations, in its assumptions, and

65

of course largely Gentile (not to say Christian) in its population, both faculty and student. This circumstance in itself would not have brought two men together, any more than it would have kept them apart. But even here, in the likeness, there was a strong element of difference.

Leon Solomon was a New York Jew. Charles winced at having to put the matter so plainly even to himself. Solomon was one of those brilliant boys of poor family who do so splendidly at college (C.C.N.Y. in this instance) that they might easily astonish the world, had they ever had an opportunity of liking it a little better, or of knowing it except through books.

Charles on the other hand, laughable as the distinction might appear, was a Connecticut Jew, and not Merritt Parkway Connecticut either, but of the small town, inland variety which resembled the Connecticut Yankee at least a good deal more than it did the Jew, whether rich or poor, of New York City. Charles, as he did not look at all like the stereotype of a Jew, had seldom needed to maintain the fact of his race against opposition, nor had he ever denied it; while Leon Solomon, in addition to his name and his nose, was blessed with a plenty of those traits which, when they appear in a Gentile, are called "loud-mouthed," "arrogant," "pushy," and so on, but in a Jew are taken by the whole world quite simply as the quintessence of Jewishness. The distinction was in the first place bitterly unfair, but one had to allow that nobody maintained it more fiercely than Solomon himself, whom Charles had heard to say, quite formally, in a faculty meeting at which faculty attendance at chapel was encouraged and solicited, "I presume that doesn't apply to little kikes like me?" As a position, it was perhaps admirable; but its tone, in a supposedly civilized community of scholars, left something to be wished; it seemed to design everyone's embarrassment with no real object at all, which seemed Mr. Solomon's regular design for living.

It was not so much, Charles thought, that Solomon did not believe what the others believed; it was rather that he would not pretend to believe what the others pretended to believe—what Charles, for the sake of peace, pretended to believe, or, less positively and more accurately, allowed himself, without difficulty, to assume: that there were no real problems as between Gentile and Jew, or none at any rate which could not be elided in the definition of both parties as *gentlemen.*

It further appeared probable that at some time in the past Leon Solomon had been a Communist, though by how strict a definition, or whether he was still (Charles thought not) had not as yet become clear. Remembering his own college days, Charles thought it quite likely that such a person as Solomon, by nature a kind of Thersites or Apemantus (perhaps with the intention of being a Socrates?), a kind of gadfly to a society in which he appeared at the time of the Spanish Civil War, should have been a member of the party, or at least of the Young Communist League. Some sufficient association of this sort had been brought up in the course of one of those meddlesome internecine investigations by means of which the College, a year ago, had thought to forestall a more public investigation; which in turn had

67

become a threatening possibility for no better reason than that Senator Stamp, a not very active or distinguished member of a committee in Washington, was an alumnus and a member of the board of trustees. A committee of the faculty had been set up (Charles was grateful for not having been asked to serve) with a power of asking questions whose answers, presuming it got any, would enable the house to be set in order without outside interference. There was in all this nothing like a loyalty oath; in fact the entire object, in practical terms, remained decently vague, and so far as Charles was aware nothing had been said about penalties, conclusions, or the legality of the business, which had scarcely been heard from again except for the small stir that was observable when Leon Solomon, pointing out that the committee had no legal right to question him, refused to answer and more or less dared President Nagel, through the committee, to do anything about it. His speech on this occasion, so it was reported by rumor as far as Charles, had contained distinct threats of lawsuits, undesirable publicity, investigation by the AAUP and perhaps the Civil Liberties Union. The matter at this moment rested inconclusively there, and Charles thought the likeliest resolution would be that Mr. Solomon, who as an instructor had no tenure, would quietly be let go at the end of the current academic year; if, as did not seem altogether probable, he would go quietly. But that was not Charles's problem.

His problem had perhaps a merely symbolic import; that is, the solution to it would have little enough practical effect on any area of the real world which Charles did not consider trivial (football); but in the definition of himself, to himself, it was a little weightier than that. Had he not, however innocently—and he did not allow that his decisions had been entirely innocent—allied himself with some rather unscrupulous forces against, as now turned out, the one man of all whom he would prefer not to have offended, precisely because he could well afford to offend him?

In any case, something must be done, even if Charles at this moment was uncertain whether he was the man to do it, or whether he had not already gone too far to the other side to be able to come back. It was a delicate point for him, because it was almost true to say that he personally did not give a damn one way or the other; almost true, but not quite. He felt that he ought to give (at least) a damn, that his principles, when not in abeyance, were sufficiently high to make him extremely uncomfortable if he didn't; at the same time, he was by now approaching the state of mind that Job's wife described so penetratingly when she advised her husband to "curse God and die." That was the sinister comfort available to even the most moral nature, perhaps especially to that nature: that when matters became confused enough, and difficult enough you could let go, even at the price of discomfort, and say to yourself, "what's the difference? It's only life," which in secular terms amounted precisely to the suggestion made by the lady to her carbuncular husband.

Charles thought that he had not quite reached that extremity as yet, and though he sighed about it, believing the explanation he felt he owed to Leon Solomon would in fact explain little, accomplish less, and command neither sympathy nor belief, he dutifully went downstairs, through the reading room—which was empty on account of the football weekend—and to the telephone.

"Philosophy, please," he said to the operator, and, to himself, while waiting, "The new philosophy calls all in doubt."

"Is Mr. Solomon around? This is Charles Osman, tell him, in History."

After a few moments Solomon got on the phone. Charles had vaguely prepared a long descriptive, and perhaps mollifying, introduction, but at the first phrases of that loud, sardonic voice it became clear that an introduction was neither necessary nor to be permitted.

"Brother, have I been hearing about you! They tell me you understand about developing the whole person, and how football is just as important to academic life as all this other crap we teach—"

"Now, really, listen, Solomon—"

"You are a Christian gentleman," the voice continued, "or practically a Christian gentleman, and a true member of the *maspocha* of educated men—whereas I, I—"

"If you're going to take that attitude—"

"Me? Me? I'm not taking an attitude, *they* are. Do you know, Asher, that what began at Pearl Harbor was finished in the Rose Bowl? That Plato said music *and* gymnastic? That Immanuel Kant invented the forward pass?"

"You're a little wrought up," Charles said.

"Poddon me," the other said with elaborate courtesy,

"I *am* wrought up. I've never been so important since my *bar mitzvah*. Why shouldn't I be wrought up? For years nobody ever cared about my mind, now all of a sudden I should change it."

"I didn't do it to you," Charles said wearily, "at least—"

"*La trahison des clercs,* chum," the voice said in a horrible French accent, and, without self-consciousness, said it again: "*La trahison des clercs.*"

"Get this straight." Charles, trying to be decisive, succeeded in being as loud as Solomon. "I did not know you were involved. Got that? I was not told until a few minutes ago that the kid flunked your course as well as mine. I'm sorry. I apologize, and if I can put things right I'll do it, if it's not too late."

"Ignorance of the law?" The voice was still jeering, but Charles thought it sounded a blessed trifle less certain of everything.

"I honestly thought it was up to me alone," Charles said. "And I haven't said the boy can play, not yet. I've said I'd see him. Now what I wanted to know is, where do you stand? Now, I mean."

"I'm not standing, I'm sitting here on my ass." And there seemed in Solomon's manner some grudging impulse to friendliness, which he must have heard himself, since he at once added: "Don't get the idea I'm relying on you, my friend. I knew when I flunked the kid that the whole business would end with me up the creek as usual. This is just an excuse, Osman. They're out to get me any way they can, you know that yourself. I just gave 'em the excuse they've been looking for."

"Isn't that just a touch paranoid, Solomon? *They,* who are *They?*"

"There's a thing Sigmund had to say about that, too," the voice replied. "With a kind of wistful look at that whole area, he said, 'The paranoid is not altogether wrong.' Think it over, chum, think it over."

"If you want me to back you up—" Charles began; but was at once interrupted.

"There's nothing I want from you," said Solomon, though in his tone there now seemed something fundamentally opposed to this plain statement, as he said in a much more distant and quieter voice, "I don't want anything from any of you. So I suffer. So what?"

"I've said I'd see Blent," Charles persisted. "Are you going to do that—see him and talk to him?"

"I am not."

"I admire your firmness, but don't you think—?"

"Spare me your admiration."

"Don't you think you're making a good deal of trouble for yourself over nothing?"

"It's a test case, Osman. Even you can see that, a test case. Here are the rules, here I am. What could be clearer? It's better the trouble should be over nothing; the principle stands out that way."

"I see. If that's the way you want it, Solomon, I'm sorry I interfered with the purity of your moral experiment, and I'll tell you again, I apologize. By the way, what course of yours did Blent fail?"

There was a pause, as though the other begrudged him even this information.

"It's called Modern Ethical Theory." The voice was sulky now; but suddenly there came a violent laugh which seemed to share the metallic nature of the telephone itself, and then: "It may help you to see the grand humor of the thing, Osman, if I tell you that the exam he flunked was on Machiavelli, just plain Machiavelli. Why, the kid ought to be teaching the course. I could sit at his feet. Maybe he is Machiavelli."

"All right," said Charles. "I understand. Don't run it into the ground."

"Probably he's Cesare Borgia, though," Solomon went on reflectively, "and I can be Machiavelli because he didn't know practical politics from a hole in the ground either; all he could do was teach."

"Well, I'm sorry," Charles said again. "I've got to go talk with the boy now." He waited for some possible gesture of reconciliation.

"I hope they raise your salary for it," was what Solomon said.

3

Perhaps Charles had overprepared himself for this meeting with Raymond Blent; at least, after that conversation with Mr. Solomon his judgment merely abdicated its function for the time being, so that when the student at last appeared Charles, who had been looking out the window of his office and musing, scarcely recognized him at first; though this was partly, it is true, on account of the fact that it had got very dark and gloomy in the office; and that, in turn, was on account of

73

the high wall of the stadium just across the way, which cut off the sun; and that, in its turn, had been the subject, or the occasion, of Charles's reverie.

The stadium had been put up only a few years ago, yet there were large cracks in the concrete already, and the wall was substantially clothed in ivy; ivy seemed to grow fast and tough in the academic atmosphere, and Charles compared this fact, in his thought, with a sentence he had once heard spoken in a Commencement oration: "Some of our traditions are old, while others are of relatively recent development . . ."

His office had been a more pleasant place before that stadium went up; it used to get the sun all afternoon (marvelous for dozing), and had a view across the level playing field (he had been able to watch football practice) to the row of faculty houses on a slight rise beyond.

But now the high bulk of the stadium intercepted the November sun from about three in the afternoon, and the view, despite the ivy, disagreeably suggested a prison, as did the wire mesh on the library window.

To the historian's mind, that edifice across the way, like all cathedrals, capitols and coliseums, appeared as the frozen resultant of many human wills; it expressed something of the spirit, of which he, remembering and deducing the process, was able to be the witness.

The College had grown very considerably since the war and during Charles's tenure there. This growth in size though not necessarily in intellectual stature had produced a period of tension about the kind and quality of football played here, which some had considered too small-time to be quite respectable. There had followed a period of "overemphasis" that became the occasion of a controversy which nearly destroyed the faculty. Either the serious academicians won, then, or else it was merely the dialectical element in the *Zeitgeist* itself; in any case, what happened next had been a period of "de-emphasis" which nearly destroyed the College. Even if one didn't like football, or considered it at best unimportant, one had to allow that had been a depressing two or three years, in which a certain spiritlessness, feeling of general failure, had spread as it were symbolically from the football squad—the Awkward Squad, after it had won only three games in two seasons—through the rest of the institution. Everyone, even the most intensely pedantic of the faculty, seemed to become bored and listless.

It seemed that by now the Hegelian synthesis, if one cared to call it that, of the two positions had led the College to an intermediate position which could be named quite simply "emphasis"; but this "emphasis," owing again to the continued growth of the place, was far greater than what would have been called "overemphasis" a few years before. And this "emphasis," by means of interminable committee meetings, secret diplomacy of all sorts, "popular movements" among the students (who later turned out to have been led by agitators enrolled in the school by certain alumni groups), had caused to arise, not without graft and a scandal resulting in the dismissal of Dr. Nagel's predecessor in the presidency, this stadium, whose present effect was to block Charles Osman's view and prevent the sunlight

75

from reaching him during the late afternoon. From its wall there reverberated also the sort of rhythmical exaltation one always associated with football weekends, and which could be traced, if Charles attended closely, to a bass drum beating a long way off.

There was a knock at the door behind him, and he turned to see the young man standing there in the dusk.

"I'll turn on the light," Charles said, and when he had done so they blinked at one another uncertainly for an instant or two.

"Sit down, Mr. Blent," he said then, and added, when he had taken his own seat, "I don't know what to say to you at all."

"I'm sorry if I've caused you a lot of bother, sir," Blent replied. "But let me say this one thing: I would not have come sucking around for favors if they hadn't forced me to. I was ready to accept the consequences of my act, Dr. Osman," he finished in a certain tone of self-conscious pride, probably (Charles thought) at that bookish phrase, "the consequences of my act."

"I believe you," Charles said; and they sat in silence for a few moments.

Charles thought Blent at least an extremely handsome boy; it would be more appropriate to call him beautiful, since his features expressed so much of fineness and delicacy, though it was delicacy on the magnificent or heroic scale. The whole head appeared to Charles as unreservedly aristocratic and, at the same time, innocent; there was also something of statuary about the modeling of the flesh; especially the lips, a trifle too thick perhaps, suggested the lofty silence of some portrait head of the Old Kingdom where the stone almost becomes flesh—here, the opposite process seemed in force, giving a hard, luminous quality to the cheeks and forehead. The eyes were gray and classically inexpressive; they gave no clue, in Charles's opinion, to any inwardness at all, while at the same time they looked intelligent. The black hair, tightly curled, also had something of the texture of stone. Blent was dressed in a blue serge suit, more formal than what he generally wore in class; it was "the best blue suit" of poverty, and it looked to Charles as if someone—Coach Hardy, maybe —had dressed the boy up in this uncomfortable style to meet his doom.

"I'll say in turn," Charles began at last, "that I've watched you play football, and I think you do it well."

"Thank you, sir."

"I was sorry to see you fail my Hour Exam, especially as it wasn't by any means a hard one."

"I failed it all the same." No trace of irony or even humor in this.

"Well, you know the situation," Charles said briskly, as though getting down to business. "I feel a little trapped, but that's not your fault, I guess, and anyhow we don't need to go into the details of it. I'll do what the forms of things require of me, and so will you—though I don't see where it will help if Mr. Solomon won't do the same, and I gather he damn well won't."

"Yes, sir."

"Mr. Blent, what was the color of Oliver Cromwell's white horse?"

"What? Oh, white."

"Okay. You can go tell Coach Hardy that you're eligible to play." Blent continued to sit there, and Charles said, "What are you waiting for, Mr. Blent? Do you want to be congratulated? I've put on the farce as commissioned, but it doesn't include a big production with real scenery. You may as well get going." But the boy did not move, and Charles found he was not in the least surprised, though somewhat exasperated—and perhaps the least bit pleased?—to see those fine gray eyes fill up with tears.

"Now what is it?" he said.

"You—despise—me," the boy brought out in a shaking voice.

"Now, please, Blent, let's not do everything the hard way. You must try to see my side in this business."

"You detest me—and you're right."

"Really, I had no such thought," Charles said. "It may be that I took out on you a little extra resentment I've had all day against—against other people. If that's how it looks to you, I'm sorry. I didn't mean to be unkind."

"You have every right to be," the boy said, and added in a stifled voice which struggled with sobs, "I've always admired and respected you, sir. I didn't think you would . . . be like this."

"Oh, that's great," said Charles broadly, "that's just grand. Be like what? A cynical outrider of the football team, you mean? You hoped I'd turn out a suffering witness to the truth, a martyr of History 124A? My dear boy, when you grow up you may begin to see some things about this world which you don't quite see at this moment. Meanwhile, I'd just as soon not discuss my character."

Blent snuffled something indistinguishable.

"Now look," Charles said, his exasperation overreaching itself and turning into a display of further generosity, "you mustn't take on in this way. Try to calm yourself. I'll do this: you go off and play football with a clear conscience, and next week sometime, when you're prepared, I'll give you a make-up exam. Fair enough?"

"You don't understand, sir." Here the voice broke, and Blent simply sobbed for a few minutes. After that, looking Charles sternly in the eye, he added, "I've done —something bad."

Charles looked sternly back.

"Ray, are you trying to tell me that you failed my test on purpose?"

The student looked suddenly hopeful.

"Ah, you guessed that—you saw it, then," he said. Charles did not feel called on to reveal that Miss Sayre was the source of his new reputation for shrewdness and understanding.

"If that's what bothers you," he said easily, "relax. I don't know why you did it, but I'll take it that you had reasons, which I won't pry into. I suppose the same thing goes for Mr. Solomon's exam?"

"But you don't know why," Blent insisted.

"As to that," said Charles, more easily, more genially than ever, "I don't need to know, do I? Maybe I could make a pretty fair guess, though, at that. A girl, something to do with a girl?"

"She's been at you, too," Blent said; the word "she" bore surprising and considerable scorn. "She doesn't know the half of it, she hasn't any notion."

There followed a long, uncomfortable silence.

"I'm not pressing you for confidences," Charles finally said, "but if it's as terrible as you make it sound, maybe you'd better tell me. Sometimes these things don't sound so awful, once they've been said out loud." But he added, "Don't unless you want to."

"I want your good opinion, sir, and your respect," the boy said very sternly; Charles felt in this a sympathetic touch of his own character. "I really mean, sir, that I've done something wrong. Unforgivably wrong. And then I went ahead and got everything mixed up worse than ever, trying to get out."

Charles waited.

"I took money to throw the game," Blent said.

The point about receiving such confessions, as Charles knew, whether one were priest or psychoanalyst or merely professor of history, was that one showed no surprise and, above all, gave no impression of being shocked or, for that matter, morally involved at all. Charles, however, was surprised, morally involved, and shocked.

"Dear name of heaven, why?" he said. Now the dreadful words had been said, he saw, Blent was past the stage of tears and able to speak plainly.

"I don't quite know why even now," he said. "I've tried to figure it out, but all my reasons are probably what anyone else would call rationalizations. There aren't any reasons for doing a thing like that," he finished glumly.

"Tell me how it happened."

"I don't know—it just happened."

"Now, look," Charles said impatiently, "you must

know something about it. It didn't happen in your sleep, did it? How much money?"

"Five hundred in advance. Fifteen hundred after we lose."

"And who gave it to you?"

"Gee, Mr. Osman, that's the trouble. I don't know."

"You don't know?"

"It was just—a man. A kind of fat man with crinkled gray hair. He was wearing a polo coat. He was a Jew, I think."

"Look here, mister," Charles said, "as a Jew myself, I resent that. Jews are not necessarily the only crooks in the world. You don't know anything about this man—but right away you know he is a Jew. That's contemptible."

"I'm sorry, sir, I didn't mean I was prejudiced, or anything. He just looked that way, is all."

"All right, then, go on."

"He offered me the money."

"Where did all this happen?"

"In my room—in the boarding house I live at."

"He offered you this money—and you simply took it. Was that how it happened?"

"No, sir. At first I thought he was joking. I was sort of uncomfortable, and I told him I ought to throw him out of my room, or report to the coach. But he said if I did that he would put it in the papers that I had already taken a bribe and then repented, and that a story like that would do me a lot of harm. And then he began to talk to me about my future, and how it was all very well to be a football player, but that there were bigger things than football in the world, and how a lot of people were making money off my talent and skill, and that it was lucky he had taken an interest in me."

"And you simply sat there with a happy smile?"

"Well—it was like some things I'd thought myself, sir," Blent said. "I've always been poor. It was like," he added rather eagerly, "it was like some things Mr. Solomon says in his class."

"Indeed. Such as?"

"That people in the modern world are divided into fools and knaves. That philosophies are merely procedures for dominating people. That we ought to be able to detect the profit motive in the loftiest ethical schemes. That in a hard world the smart man prepares himself to believe nothing, keep up appearances, and make money."

"You are aware, Raymond, that there are other views? And that the ones you have repeated are not even especially original? Didn't it occur to you, either, that Mr. Solomon's precepts and his example are far apart?"

"Well, I don't know, sir," the boy said with some sullen heat. "Do you expect us to hear what you teachers tell us just for kicks? I want some practical value out of my education."

"You sure seem to've got it now," said Charles. "So you took the money?"

"Not then. We just talked about what I could do if I did take it. He wanted to know if, for example, I could be bad without looking bad, if I could fall down on the job without getting yanked out of the game. I said I thought I could, and he asked if there was any way I

82

could see to it, on my own, that the other boys were better than twelve points ahead at the finish. I said there was some chance they could do that without my help, and he said in that case I was earning the easiest buck he'd ever heard of. I said I didn't like that kind of thing, and he told me to grow up and see what the world was about."

"Twelve points?" said Charles.

"Yes. Then—this is the hard part to understand, sir—I just laughed and said I'd do it. And just at that moment, you know, I felt happy as all hell, kind of crazy-happy, tense, like waiting for the first kick-off. And he said I'd better be sure of myself, because he didn't like a man who welched on a deal. And I said—because I suddenly saw everything turned upside down, because I was saying 'go die' to the whole world for the first time—I said I was sure. We shook hands."

"And?"

"The money came by registered mail next day while I was out. My landlady signed for it." Blent reached into his pocket and drew forth a fat wallet; he put a wad of twenty-dollar bills on the desk.

"You didn't keep the envelope?"

"I burned it. I was getting nervous as all hell by then, and feeling sick inside, and I didn't know what to do, but I was afraid somebody might find that envelope and begin to suspect something, I don't know what—it was just a plain, typed envelope—so I burned it."

"Well," said Charles. "I don't know if you've flunked Modern Ethical Theory or passed it with high honors. Is there any damn reason, do you think, why I shouldn't

83

turn you in—to the administration, if not to the police?"

"No, sir."

"Do you have any alternative suggestions?"

"I would have given the money back—I know that. But I couldn't find this man, I had no way of looking for him."

"So you thought the graceful way out was to flunk a course—two courses, for good measure—and get made ineligible?"

"Yes, sir."

"It must have seemed an inspired move. But now you find the world is really against you, that everyone is ready to break all the rules in your favor, just so you can play and lose—which you don't want to do."

"That's about it."

Charles considered all this in silence for a minute or so.

"It would be a slight understatement to say that your position is equivocal," he said. "Do you feel you want to suffer and be punished?"

"I said I respect you, sir," said Blent. "I mean that. I'm relieved you know—I'd rather you knew than anyone—and I'm willing to abide by your decision."

"Thanks so much," said Charles wryly. "It'd be Christlike if I said 'go sin no more,' but human beings are not required to take that kind of responsibility; besides, what about sinning this time? We're not over that yet, it seems to me."

"I'd give anything," Blent said, leaving it unclear what he would give anything for.

"If you played tomorrow, would you play to win?"

"Yes, sir, I promise you that."

"You don't need to promise me, Ray. I don't see anyone but yourself that you can promise anything to at all. Suppose you played to win, and your team still lost, and by more than twelve points—then what?"

"This much I can promise you, sir—I'll throw the money in the guy's face when he comes back."

"But isn't it probable he won't give you that chance? That it will come by mail again?"

Blent thought about this for a while.

"I'll turn it over to you, sir," he said. "And for a start, here's the five hundred. I haven't touched any of it."

"What shall I do with it?" asked Charles. "Establish a football scholarship?"

"You could give it to charity, couldn't you? I wish," Blent wistfully added, "I could find the man and push it down his throat."

"Suppose now that you played tomorrow and won—don't you think your unknown friend would take a serious view of that? It seems to me you'd be lucky to get off with a beating up, some dark night after you'd given up expecting it."

Blent looked actually fervent about this prospect.

"That's at least one way I can prove my good faith to you, sir," he said. "I can accept that risk."

"Dammit, Ray," Charles said grumpily. "I know I ought to turn you in, ruin your future such as it is, make damn well certain of your being expelled in disgrace. I can't. And the thing I resent most is that I am the one

85

who has to decide. If I don't give you away, even that's not enough, I have to be actively on your side. I shall have to go to Solomon and force some kind of consent out of him."

"I hope you won't tell Mr. Solomon, sir," Blent said.

"Why not? He'd probably be proud of you."

"Still . . ."

"Ray, get it through your head you can't dictate anything to me. I must do whatever seems right when I come to it. As for this money—" Charles indicated the pile of bills on the desk—"I'll take charge of it for now; though damned if I know what's to be done about that eventually. We'll have to see how the game comes out, I guess. I've a sort of idea about disposing of it, but you're not to think about that now. You can go and say that so far as I'm concerned you are eligible to play. What's done about Solomon is another thing, but I have an idea that people are leaning on him pretty heavily —they'll probably find a rule somewhere saying that in cases of emergency the football coach can overrride a faculty decision."

"Sir, I want to thank you for giving me this chance." The tears which again filled Blent's eyes seemed to Charles in this instance the tears of easy and dishonest sentimentality.

"Don't talk to me that way," he said sharply, experiencing a sort of revulsion from all that he had been put through during the day, and even from himself. "Let's be quite clear about this one thing, Blent. You've behaved very badly. If I have to go along with things as they are, from where I happen to find them, that doesn't exactly make us bosom friends. I'll go this far, that I hope this sorry business works out with no serious damage to your body or your reputation; but that's all. And when it's over, if it does so work out—or even if it doesn't—I should prefer that our personal acquaintance not continue. Do you understand that?"

Blent stood up facing Charles during this speech.

"I'm sorry, sir," he said gulping and again on the verge of tears.

"You can go now," Charles said.

"I swear to you, sir," the boy said with a dramatic gasp and sob, "if we lose tomorrow, I won't go on living. I'll kill myself."

"Knock it off. You won't do anything of the kind," said Charles angrily. "Don't go around swearing things you don't mean—and especially don't swear them to me. Now go, will you? I've had enough."

"You don't believe me," cried Blent bitterly, "but you'll see. I swear." He left on this note, without attempting to shake hands.

Charles, alone, picked up the money. His fingers were trembling, and the last remarks he had made began to seem to him the vilest and most reprehensible thing about the whole affair; as though by helping the boy he had entitled himself to an arrogant moral superiority, the very vice of all which this tentative, kindly, and ironic person hated most in the world.

4

It was nightfall when Charles left the library, and the weather had turned cold again; a band of pure blue last light lay across the hills westward, where one star shone, and all else was dark. The night would bring frost and the next day probably would be fine, in support of the local belief that it never rained on Homecoming Weekend. It was the sort of evening to make anyone out walking alone much aware of the contrast between loneliness and society, outdoors and indoors. Charles's way—he was going home to change and freshen up for the President's party—took him out of the Oval, whose various Gothic and Grecian constructions, improved by darkness, rose up mysteriously among naked trees on every side, and up a couple of blocks of a street occupied by fraternity houses, all of them brilliantly alight and producing already continuously merry noises and sounds of singing. The street was lined on both sides with parked cars; driveways were filled up also; occasionally a door would open, producing as in a picture frame a sudden, yellow-bright space in which shadows leaned, moved, shouted; then the door would slam shut again.

Despite the fact that as a faculty member he had been invited to several of these functions, and would have been officially welcomed at any of them, Charles allowed himself to feel the luxurious pathos of the lonely man excluded; which had always appeared to him as *his* role no matter how many parties he was invited or even went to. It was not at all an unpleasant feeling, and its apparent seriousness gave him the impression, which he knew to be false, that he was occupied in thinking deeply as he walked.

In truth, he did not want to think; and perhaps also,

for all his being involved in a "situation"—one of those nasty crises which in the academic world no less than in others sent people scurrying about ignominiously for the sake of "discussing things"—there was at this moment little or nothing for him to think about. He seemed to be committed, though by now he had become chary of the belief that he realized the full extent of his commitment. In any case, he wanted a rest. He was experiencing the reaction which told him that he had already said too many things to too many people during the day; while at the same time he foresaw the disagreeable necessity, in consequence of that, of saying a great deal more, to the same people and others.

Charles had always felt some distaste for the sort of person who, out of some deep loneliness probably, reveled in the political occasion, the time that made it necessary to speak to this one and that one; and who at such a time went about with ill-disguised glee gathering the consolations of a society which for business reasons could not be refused. This sort of man, who is by no means a rarity among college teachers, not merely enjoyed "situations"—in Charles's opinion he went a good way toward creating them by his own impluse to expand and deepen the most trivial questions, to go far and wide gathering remotest implications and making it impossible for anyone else to remain aloof. Yet now, it seemed, Charles himself had become nearly indistinguishable from such a person, for whom everything was political, and who would say nothing which did not bear upon "the problem," "the situation," "the crisis"—and nothing, therefore, which did not have a double intention, a secret as well as an overt meaning. Only his own character and personal bearing, he now felt, could save him from being the sort of man into whose situation he had been thrust by force of circumstance—and could he honestly say that circumstance was alone responsible?

He did not see how he could in reason have behaved otherwise than as he had except in one way, that is, by a cold and rigid adherence to the letter of the law, a mode of conduct which he did not admire, and which, in his view, made one's decisions moral (and therefore safe) but at the cost of their ethical content. It began to seem, however, that in this instance the letter and the spirit might be, as they were never said to be, one.

He turned back to the right now, past the black height of the stadium which lay at a little distance, the intervening space being occupied by various practice fields; at his left ranged a row of faculty dwellings, in one of which, some little way along, he lived.

Some cars were drawn up in a square on the practice fields, their headlights illuminating a central space where a large tower of logs was being raised. Around this bonfire there would be a Pep Rally later in the evening, where speeches were spoken and songs sung and cheers cheered; where, in the manner of antiquity (or the manner of savages), the generated spirit of crusade received its ritual blessing and the troops were incited to valor. Ridiculous, no doubt, and, to the civilized intelligence, repulsive as well; but precisely because, ridiculous and repulsive, the thing worked. The people who gathered round that blaze later on, the plebs (to recall President Nagel's illuminating comparison), would really feel exaltation and awe, and so for that matter might such of their elders and betters as attended. There would be the feeling of enormous force concentrated and available at one place and one time, there would be the feeling of great though mysterious significance reaching deep into the real nature of things; and such feelings, though the result largely of lies and deceitful truths, were by no means altogether false: the rain dance did not really bring the rain, perhaps, but it brought the tribe to the pitch of enthusiasm at which they really at any rate planted the corn; and it ought not to be overlooked, either, that the rain dance was danced at the beginning of the rainy season, and not in the dry.

Charles stopped for a moment to watch the students who climbed in stages the sides of that already tall Tower of Babel and handed up the light wood used for filler. These were the stagehands, the base mechanicals who in every enterprise of the kind labored long hours to ensure that at the appropriate moment the god would descend in his machine among choirs of angels.

No doubt society—civilization, if it could be said to be—consisted more largely than people generally cared to admit in these gatherings and releasings of energy, whose significance must be called *symbolic*, a mysterious word which meant, most often, that nobody knew the meaning of the phenomenon to which it was applied. No doubt, too, a civilization might be summed up as the parody of its myths; even a bonfire such as this one referred, though unconsciously, to endings and

91

beginnings, to the universal conflagration and the re-
newal of time, but it didn't matter, and perhaps would
matter very little, after all, if the entire College also
went up in smoke, or if the world did.

It seemed to him, as he walked along, that one thing
at least might be said for "situations," that at the cost of
some inconvenience they placed the historian, when he
participated, in a privileged position. For if history
consisted, as he had only that morning told his class
not for the first time, of an inside and an outside, he now
stood, with respect to this small history of only and
doubtful symbolic import, on the problematic border
between inside and outside; where he could regard
grand effects produced by mean causes, where "the
herald's cry, the soldier's tread," were to be seen as no
less potent and no less poignant than before, although
produced in their fullest resonance by chicanery in
closed rooms, and the doubtful motives of private persons. The idea that the Homecoming Game, the center
of all this logistical fuss, movement of supplies and
people, the blaze of one real decision among so many
formalities, should have been fixed—and even now one
could not be sure it was not, nor under the circumstances could one ever be sure again—this idea struck
Charles as the sad joke, the saddest of all, which seems
to the teller uproariously funny but which everyone else
considers to be in the worst possible taste (not that, as
things presently stood, he planned on telling anyone).
It was the joke emblematic of history, perhaps, and the
one, accordingly, which historians and philosophers

skirted most carefully around the edges of when laying out their glorious systems.

It was this same joke, apparently, which Mr. Solomon, even without direct inward knowledge of this particular situation, correctly placed at the center of his admittedly rather jejune teaching. But Charles warned himself severely against accepting any student's version of the content of any course; no doubt those gems which Blent had given in such isolated prominence had been, in the actual delivery in class, surrounded with variations, cautions, ifs and buts, to a degree that the boy was unable or unwilling to take in; besides, Blent had been merely looking for justifications.

The problem now was, what (if anything) to do about Solomon. Charles thought he could put off a decision on this subject until he had spoken to President Nagel; perhaps that part of the affair had already been settled without his help. Meanwhile, he very much wished there were someone he might talk to, not with absolute candor (which was out of the question) but with at any rate some freedom; someone who, like himself, might in part be presumed to be both inside and outside this sordid business. It did not escape him, however, that if he thought at once of Lily Sayre it was not because she ideally met these terms, but merely because he wanted very much to see her again. So he phoned her home in town as soon as he got in. Some woman, perhaps a maid, asked his name and said Miss Sayre had left a number for him; though her motive in doing this could be accountable purely to "the situation" Charles was nevertheless pleased. He called the number given, and out of a gaggle of voices, as though a party were being held in the phone booth, one shouted in answer to his request that it would try to find Miss Sayre; which presently it must have done.

"I want to talk to you," Charles said.

"I'm glad you called," she replied. "It's noisy here, though."

"Where are you?"

"Oh—this is Alpha Sigma. Why don't you come here?"

"I've got to talk to you alone," Charles said, wondering why he thought he must do that. "And I'm busy for an hour now. Could you eat dinner with me later?"

"I shouldn't do that," she said. "There're these people I'm with . . . Ray isn't here, of course."

"I didn't want to have dinner with Ray," said Charles. "I've something odd to tell you, not on the phone."

"I *could*, I guess," she answered. "Call for me here in, say, an hour and a half."

Charles hung up, then called the Aaron Burr and reserved a table.

"And listen," he said to Mr. Giardineri. "What we talked about at noon today—do you know those people, those big-money operators?"

"What's on your mind, Doc?" the other asked cautiously.

"I mean, could you find one of 'em for me?"

"Oh, I don't know about that, sir." Mr. Giardineri had grown suddenly much more distant, as though he were denying someone a reservation.

94

"Try to know, please—it's important," Charles said. "A favor. I'll tell you more about it when I get there."

"Such things are not easy to arrange. Even if I knew those people—which I don't admit."

"See what you can do for me," Charles said. "I promise you I'm not in this to make trouble."

"In some places, Professor," Mr. Giardineri said, "trouble makes itself without your help." He hung up.

Charles shaved again, even though he had done so that morning, and dressed with somewhat more care, perhaps, than he would have done for the President's cocktail party alone. While he shaved, he examined his face carefully in the mirror and found it attractive— ruggedly handsome, you might say (he said), and showing no signs of middle age, only the decisive dignity of experience intelligently received. By the time he had finished dressing and walked from the bedroom into the parlor of his small apartment—the house was divided into several such, for bachelor members of the faculty —he was prepared to allow a certain want of true comfort in the somewhat nomadic style of his furnishings; and glancing twice at the portrait of his late wife which still stood on his desk, he remarked in passing that he had formed the tentative intention of marrying Miss Lily Sayre.

The portrait of course did not reply, unless by a slight intensification of its disconcertingly steady glance, and Charles, pleased with his resolve, left it in the dark and went down to get out his car and drive to the President's house.

3

At the party in the President's house was concentrated the real and unobtrusive power of the academic community, a small, select assemblage of *eminences grises* which made President Nagel himself feel uncomfortably like a flat figure on a weathervane, some emblematic rooster who faces with great authority, and seems to direct, the wind that turns him. In this gathering he was the newcomer, the interloper of a few years' standing only. Even the emeritus professor of geology, who in his retirement (which had already lasted an incredible twenty years) raised Pekingese, and who had to be attended on his rare excursions by a trained nurse, counted for far more around here than Nagel could ever hope to do; while the professor in his turn was eclipsed by certain members of the board and one or two alumni now present, who could if they cared to (and they might, they might) buy the College and turn it into an experimental sheep farm or a Jesuit novitiate or a country club. For these persons a college president was quite simply a man one hired to run things, like a janitor, as Nagel had suggested that morning to Charles Osman. Oh, he had no doubt his dignity and his authority—without these things he would have been worthless—but his having them was a matter obscurely conditional, and his keeping them was decided where, when, how, on what grounds? On such occasions as this he was keenly aware of not belonging here, of having come here more or less by accident and remaining more or less on sufferance. He would have liked to say to himself that he did not care, but that would no longer be quite true. His being here, even on these terms, was success, and beyond expectation; he thought he could do a good job, and would like to stay. Just now, though, he could detect a slight smell of crisis in the air, some tension as yet problematic but trivial which did not look as though it could seriously affect his position—one couldn't tell, though, about that!—but which brought up all his latent doubts about his background and even his character.

He had managed to gather one important thing about football during the past few years: that these people, his trustees and some of the most influential of his graduates, had intense feelings which centered around this game, and that they were perhaps a trifle ashamed of having these feelings; that is, they carefully, even self-consciously, avoided any enthusiasm of the rah-rah sort, the banner and the coonskin coat left over from their college days in a strong smell of mothballs, but if the subject had to be faced squarely they became serious, as they might do in a discussion of their religious faith or their patriotism. The College's present status in the sport had not been arrived at merely in the course of nature, but represented a long-term program (it had begun before his arrival, with the decision to build the stadium) having to do about equally with morale and money. Building the stadium was a courageous and far-sighted decision (Nagel had been told on being hired) which, however, meant nothing without the follow-through: you had to keep the stadium filled. If you kept the stadium filled, the bonds would be paid off in a matter of five years; if the bonds were paid off, everything after that was gravy (this frivolous expression had not been used, actually), and it was felt by certain alumni groups that *ultimately*—a courageous and far-sighted word—the financial strain upon such groups might be considerably eased and the entire College become, to a degree almost beyond the respectable, self-supporting. Moreover, this result would bring with it a handsome dividend in morale and reputation: you would get more students—statistics were advanced to show they would be better students—and you might eventually be able to turn the College into a university, since you would be able to attract (the following phrase had actually been used) "a higher type money."

98

Harmon Nagel had acquiesced before being hired in this line of reasoning; he would dearly love to see the College turn into a university under his visible responsibility, and he had proposed simply to the members of the board, being courageous and far-sighted in his turn, that the university, when it came, would include among its first departments the goal of his own dream, a graduate school of divinity; this suggestion had been met with grave approval.

Dr. Nagel in no sense believed himself to have contracted with the powers of darkness in making such arrangements; and he was a man who took the powers of darkness with some seriousness. As a general rule, the scheme had gone forward much as it might have without him, and at no cost to his conscience. As a matter of fact, not a little had been done to protect the sensibilities of the academic world; the establishment of a program of athletic scholarships was hedged around with restrictions about grades in high school, aptitude tests, personality tests, with stringent rules about traveling expenses, volunteer recruitment, and competitive bidding against other institutions of learning; when the player arrived at college he was to find that his studies, under the rules on eligibility (which now seemed to be at issue), had a priority even over football. Nor had Coach Hardy been foisted on the President as a big-time, high-pressure operator; Dr. Nagel had chosen the man himself from among three candidates presented by alumni nomination, and his choice had been guided by his impression of Hardy's character, that of one who promised no spectacular results, was willing to regard

99

himself as a member of the faculty, and saw football in proportion with other activities, as playing a part in the development of "the all-round man" (a phrase rather popular among educators in those days).

Under the circumstances, perhaps the only thing about the athletic program which made Dr. Nagel uneasy was its success. However it had come about, in a few years since his taking up the position, Coach Hardy had fashioned teams which did the job, and did it progressively better each season, and did it in a style which combined, according to the newspapers, brilliance of conception with efficiency of execution and real teamwork, reflecting "a sound grasp of fundamentals." Dr. Nagel wondered if the same could be said for any other department in the College: did the English Department teach a sound grasp of fundamentals? Could the philosophers teach anything like brilliance of conception? Last week's explosion in the Chem Lab, which mercifully hurt no one, surely did not suggest efficiency of execution.

And now they stood on the verge, possibly, of an undefeated season; there had been a letter last week from a chamber of commerce somewhere in the South detailing plans for the inauguration, next year, of the Oil Bowl, and tentatively proposing an invitation. Well, they could cross that bowl when they came to it. Meanwhile—

Meanwhile, Dr. Nagel felt nervous.

Though no one, perhaps, was aware of it, the tone of the Nagels' cocktail party was established by the President's wife. Molly Nagel, a gray, untidy woman not in the best of health (she had nervous headaches), had long felt some discomfort of mind over the nagging thought that she had not kept up with her husband in the rise of his fortunes, that she might even be said to have let him down. Surely this college, of which he had become president so suddenly and out of a blue sky a few years back, was very different from anything they had been through together before; and he too had become different, but had she?

This place, for one thing, could be called, must be called, an old, Eastern college. With respect to both adjectives, it was on the edge, but the old and eastern edge. She (and Harmon too, for that matter) had come out of a very different, though still academic, environment. They had met while still undergraduates at a small college in Iowa, and been married immediately after commencement. Harmon had done his graduate work at the State University, and then returned to his Alma Mater to teach the History of Religion & Ethics, and in the course of fifteen years had risen, rather dramatically there too, to occupy the only endowed chair that institution possessed, the Professorship of Christian Ethics; thence, a few years after, he had accepted an invitation to the presidency of a Baptist college in Kentucky—and what a decision that had been! How they had weighed together the value and meaning of that change in their lives. At that time Harmon still considered the possibility of being ordained minister, and the debate which so occupied them then had to do with the question whether a proper humility of spirit, coupled with real dedication to the service of humanity, might not be more easily attained in the relatively modest post of teacher than in the hierarchy of administration and authority with all its attractions of dignity and worldly glory.

They had chosen worldly glory, such as it was, and the heavenly rebuke seemed to follow with piquant immediacy. The Baptist college in Kentucky was on the edge of failure, its endowment nearly gone, its current funds badly mishandled, perhaps rather from inefficiency than in any criminal way, and the best that could be said for the place from a Christian point of view was that it seemed as poor in spirit as could be desired. When Harmon assumed the presidency there, he had to face not only this poverty but, almost at once, the temptation to redeem it by evil means. Some frightful old man in the neighborhood offered not merely to put things straight but positively to assure the security of the college for many years to come, on the one condition that it would make its curricular wisdom available to none but "one hundred per cent white Protestant Americans."

Harmon, she was glad to say, had resisted, refused, and done so cheerfully, with a phrase from Luke and a charming smile: "And the devil, taking him up into an high mountain, shewed unto him all the kingdoms of the world in a moment of time . . . If thou therefore wilt worship me, all shall be thine." That refusal, as is the way of things in the world, provoked a split in the faculty and in the board of trustees which merely made more certain the demise of the college.

But out of evil good may come, and Harmon Nagel's

spirited stand in this matter made the newspapers, and might have been the one factor which more than any other caused him to be offered the presidency he now occupied, about the acceptance of which there had been between them no debate at all. And here Harmon had mightily changed, or so at any rate it seemed to his wife.

Manners were very different here, less easygoing perhaps in a way less serious, certainly less devout. Harmon was required to "meet people"—Molly's emphasis in this phrase made it plain that both words had a special intention—and to go about lecturing to alumni groups, and to make radio talks (television appearances too, more recently), and while he was in residence they had to entertain a good deal more than they had ever done before. They had, it is true, a lovely Georgian house provided them, with servants paid by the College, and a special fund, by no means small, for parties and dinners to distinguished Friends of the Red and White (as they were called), with student waiters and bartenders sent by the undergraduate employment service for the larger occasions. All this had required not merely a change in the way they lived, but even the growth of a positive new personality; at all of which Harmon excelled and she did not.

In her innocence not precisely attuned to the cocktail party as a social means, Molly began by getting drunk, which she did easily, and having to be put away from such entertainments as quietly as possible before they were over. In reaction, she now did not drink at all, and took perhaps insufficient interest in that aspect of her duty as hostess; with the result that the President's entertainments had come to be considered somewhat ascetic. This at any rate she had resolved to remedy on the present occasion, and had laid out a quantity of liquor sufficient to lay out the number invited to consume it; in emphasis of this intention she provided also a set of old-fashioned glasses about the size of the pails which children use at the seashore, only without handles; and cocktail glasses to match. She supervised the student bartenders at their work all that afternoon (the martinis and Manhattans were to be refrigerated for several hours, so that the ice should not much dilute them), and to the proportions outlined in the back of Mrs. Rombauer's cookbook she saw to it that the most generous interpretation was applied. With somewhat hard expressions of girlish glee, expressions which remained over from that 4-H bloom of other days, she exhorted her student helpers merrily and in secret to give the guests "what for" and make this party "one to remember."

In some sense, no doubt, Molly was taking an obscure revenge on this unfamiliar society by catering to its weaknesses and putting temptation in the way; but of any such motive she was unaware, and assumed she felt happy because Harmon was clearly happy, very much in his element as he stood just at the entrance to the living room, in the archway, talking with one of the trustees, Herman Sayre, and Senator Josiah Stamp, but keeping one eye and one foot in the hall ready to welcome the next arrivals. The large room was already crowded, smoky, and noisy, and the three student waiters going about with trays to provide fresh drinks and remove the empties had to be skillful going through tight places.

Harmon Nagel, for his part, was nervous. The matter of one football player might be trivial—could not have been more so, in his view—but by the growth of circumstances during the day the mere fact of its being trivial in the first place had made it important. There were, as he had said earlier to Charles Osman, pressures on him, and that they were pressures too absurd to consider seriously did not make them any lighter. The argument he had advanced against these pressures, that one football player made little difference, was too trivial to make a fuss over even if he happened to be the best football player around, had rapidly been turned against him. "If it's so damn trivial," Senator Stamp had said, "why can't the kid play? What is there against it, if it doesn't matter?"

That was the first unforeseen, unforeseeable pressure. President Nagel could have withstood, and was willing to, the ordinary grumblings of delegations of indignant undergraduates, the dire mutterings from the Director of Athletics, the sour prophecies of future suffering which came from the Public Relations Office and the Alumni Secretary; but it had turned out that young Mr. Blent came from the same village as Senator Josiah Stamp, who had made a point of traveling all the way up here from Washington simply to see the home-town boy make good. Not only so, but Senator Stamp, in one of his grandiose gestures to the grassroots, had gone to some trouble and expense to get Blent's mother and father (who had been separated for many years), provide them with transport and accommodation in town, and see to it that they came as his guests to sit in his box and watch their son play his final game. A Senator of the United States was not easily denied, especially after one had gone to the trouble of explaining that the subject of his request (or command) was, after all, unimportant. "Well, Harmon, you'll fix it up for me, then," the Senator had said, with no rising inflection.

President Nagel reflected patiently but wearily that if a man's business was making laws, and his position such that he constantly saw how such and such a piece of legislation might be changed altogether by no more than the tone of a Senator's voice, he might come to have a rather low regard for the permanence and absolute validity of such devices as laws; at any rate Senator Stamp appeared perfectly incredulous of the idea that a rule about ineligibility might with any particular firmness stand between himself and the gratification of his wish.

Now, this evening, it further appeared that Herman Sayre, for other reasons, took the same short way with the law; and if the Senator was merely a generalized form of power, who would blow off a good deal of steam but mercifully in two days be gone, Herman was local and concentrated and permanent power: member of the board, local citizen, so very rich that people willingly overlooked his behavior when drunk, as he frequently was; generous to the College, by fits and starts—had he not simply *given*, out of his own pocket, the hockey rink with refrigerating plant?—and likely to

106

leave the place something really handsome and substantial when he went.

Sayre, when he came in this evening, went straight to President Nagel and the point. "My girl—" he meant his daughter—"My girl tells me there's some fuss about Ray Blent's not playing in the game. I promised her it would be fixed up."

When Dr. Nagel said that 'fixing it up' was not so simple as all that, though he was trying, Mr. Sayre did not argue but simply said, "I promised Lily. I can't let my girl down, can I?" Then he added, "She thinks she's going to marry this boy. She won't, but I can't go back on my word, not on a little thing like this."

At that point Nagel began to feel seriously perturbed, and to wonder if, after all, he had handled Charles Osman exactly as he ought. Until then he had taken a cheerful and modest pride in that morning's demonstration of political art, and regarded Charles with the admiring condescension a surgeon might feel for a patient saved by spectacular skill on the operating table, whose life is a testimonial not merely to the surgeon but to the medical art as well.

In that entire interview, Harmon Nagel believed, he had said nothing dishonest; in effect, he had said nothing, but worked according to a kind of dialectical jiu-jitsu of which the first and only principle was to make the opponent use his own weight against himself: if he pushes forward, you lean backward, and so on. How well he had judged his man, and how fully he had realized and exploited the one great weakness in what might be termed the teaching character generally, that is, the propensity—the compulsion, even—to explain oneself, whether it was necessary or not, endlessly; to see all sides to every question; to invent compelling arguments for the other side (it all came from dealing with students, who could not invent those arguments themselves), and thus, at last, in the most reasonable way in the world, to convince oneself of what one did not, would not, and never could believe.

That all this was so, curiously, did not lessen Dr. Nagel's respect for Charles; perhaps, even, increased it. It would not have taken that intelligent man long after leaving the President's office to analyze the results of their conversation and discover himself to have dug his own pit and fallen into it. He did not believe Charles would hold that against him, or not seriously anyhow. And he thought Charles could be counted on to play his part, once he had cast himself in it, like a gentleman.

But if he had said nothing dishonest, neither had the President been completely honest; there was the little sin of omission having to do with the presence in the situation of Leon Solomon. When it became clear that Charles had not considered that, knew nothing of it, and believed himself to be at the fulcrum of the balance, Dr. Nagel had simply allowed him to continue as he was, and quickly formulated the plan of bringing Charles's acquiescence to bear upon Solomon—a plan which thus far had not worked and showed no sign of working. On this head, Nagel felt particularly confused just now: on the one hand, he thought Charles might be persuaded to have a heart-to-heart talk with Mr.

Solomon, thus averting (perhaps) the necessity of direct presidential intervention; on the other hand, he hoped with some foreboding that Charles had not learned as yet how disingenuously he had been treated, a circumstance of which the President could not help feeling a trifle ashamed.

So now, as he talked with Sayre and Stamp, to whom he had just outlined the present posture of affairs and the probable influence on it of Charles Osman's expected arrival, Dr. Nagel kept teetering back on his heels to peer down the hall, ostensibly keeping a watch for any guests and all, but really thinking only that it was time Charles came. He would like to have this ridiculous business settled once for all; and it crossed his mind that not impossibly, before the evening ended, the chips would be down and he would find himself defending the decisions of his faculty—how he wished it were anyone but that man Solomon!— against these two enraged potentates. The results of a crisis like that were probably incalculable; they were to a degree thinkable, but not pleasant to think about; they might take a year or two revealing themselves (his own contract had a year to run after the present year), but reveal themselves they very likely would, in the fullness of time.

Harmon Nagel regarded himself as an honest man; scrupulous, was the word he thought of, and its etymology, which seemed to describe a person bothered by a pebble in his shoe, suggested to him now that his honesty had become trivial, a matter of comfort only, and that perhaps he was not an honest man at all but simply a respectable one, concerned in the present matter not with what was right but with what could be made to look right: a Pharisee, and a whited sepulcher.

"Charles ought to be here by now," he said. "May I get you gentlemen another drink?"

"What about this other fellow, this Solomon?" said Herman Sayre. "Haven't I heard something about him?"

"Ah," the President said vaguely, taking the glasses. "I don't know. He's been with us only a year or so. Philosophy. Fine intellect, I've heard, fine intellect." And he moved off in search of a waiter.

"Jewish name, ain't it," Mr. Sayre said neutrally.

"Yes, Solomon and Sheba, in the Bible, must be, I should think." The Senator cleared his throat for a pronouncement: "I've got nothing against the Jewish race," he said.

It was during this time, while the President was away from his post, that Charles Osman came in, gave his hat and coat to the maid and advanced into the living room past Mr. Sayre and Senator Stamp, neither of whom he had met before. Consequently it was several minutes before the President became aware of his having appeared on the scene. Charles meanwhile got a drink from a student in a white coat, and paid his respects to his hostess. Molly Nagel looked at him doubtfully. She could not recall having invited him; only the older faculty members had been considered presentable enough to drink with the trustees; and particularly, on Senator Stamp's account, she and Harmon had resolved to exclude any and all of those young and pushing social scientists who so desperately wanted to meet someone in Washington before the next war— could this Osman be one of those? Nothing could be done about it now, if he were. But she must speak to Harmon about possible gate-crashers among his faculty.

"Delighted you could come," she said to Charles, who understood quite well the sort of thought that was going through her head. Actually, they had met a couple of times at large functions; and he had dined here once years ago, in the first term of Nagel's incumbency; but there seemed no point in reminding the lady of that.

"Thank you for having invited me, ma'am," he said gravely, and moved away.

Looking about him in the crowd, Charles saw an unprepossessing collection of old gentlemen and their frumpish ladies; yet, he reflected, it was an interesting party if one knew something of its insides. It was one of those rare occasions in the year on which a member of the teaching profession, an old enough established member, anyhow, could be afforded a formal inspection of his results. And returning alumni, he supposed, had the same chance of looking over, after the lapse of twenty or thirty years, those brilliant young instructors whom they had so admired, feared, or detested that the memory had become legend.

As a general rule, there was no problem in distinguishing the former student, male or (occasionally) female, and the trustee, from the professor, for all in the first categories had come dressed formally, with the evident intention of going on to a dinner afterward; while the teachers for the most part betrayed by their clothing that they had nowhere to go but home. This social distinction was not quite absolute: three or four old academic gentlemen wore dinner clothes, which had, however, a greenish tinge about the lapels and did not fit as well as they might. Yet that distinction of dress was neither the only nor the most important one; another, more basic perhaps, worked in the opposite way.

For it was entertaining to see that on one side, shabby, a little stooped, tentative in gesture, ironic in speech, stood the world of intellectual dignity; and that it still, after so many years, frightened the other side a little, in a relation which both sides, probably, enjoyed. These successful bankers, lawyers, manufacturers, treated their former teachers with considerable respect—a temporary respect, thought Charles, based on a long-term contempt—in which was, perhaps, something of bewilderment; as though to say, "Here they are still, after all those years in which we made money and they didn't. They must have been getting something out of it— what could it have been?"

Here was the emeritus professor of geology, for example, old as the rocks on which he lectured, who was seriously expounding to two delighted fifty-year-old undergraduates—they still called him "Roxy," naturally—on the intellectual deficiencies which had made it clear from the beginning that they were doomed to be vice-presidents forever.

"Of course I flunked you, Kirby," he was saying in his gentle but high-pitched voice. "If you had bothered to ask me on the second day of term I could have told you that you didn't have it and wouldn't get it."

Mr. Kirby, apoplectic and bifocal, was visibly happy at this attention; at the same time, nudging his companion and speaking rather loud as though their vis-à-vis were deaf, he said, "See. He remembers. Old Roxy never forgot a thing in his life."

"It is scarcely a credit to me," the old man said. "He remembered Kirby; what an epitaph."

This remark and its acceptance on the other side, Charles thought, summed up the relation. The old man did not care if he gave offense, but there was, there could be, no offense taken, since Kirby did not really believe the professor of geology to be a human being but, much rather, an element in his own past, a deity dispossessed but still personally a trifle frightening, a clever arrangement for smiling and talking and remembering Kirby. It was funny, perhaps also it was sad.

Charles turned and put his empty glass on a tray held out by a student waiter; he took another. Something in the cut of the white coat caused him to look at the face above it. Young Mr. da Silva was smiling at him rather knowingly.

"Honesty holding out, sir?" the young man asked.

"Ah, the boy *Gauleiter* in disguise," said Charles. "Have you got me in trouble yet?"

"Who wants trouble? Anyhow, I hear everything is all right."

"You hear a good deal," Charles said. "So far as I know, nothing is all right."

"Listen, Mr. Osman, if I said anything personal this morning I didn't mean it, you know that. Just a move in the game, you know?"

"I accept your apology," said Charles, "but don't get the idea it was you and your fat friend that moved all those mountains—if they've been moved."

"I don't want the credit," Da Silva said with cheerful impudence. "You got convinced, though, hey? By him?" He nodded his head toward President Nagel in the far corner.

"Now look here," Charles said angrily, "you'd do well to keep out of this, son. I'm not accountable to you for my actions, and I haven't any great regard for your opinion of me, but I will say this: you are judging a situation that you don't know much about."

"Ah, Mr. Osman, I'm not blaming you. Every man's got to go with the tide now and then. A little compromise here and there keeps the wheels turning."

Charles looked at the student sternly, realizing at the same time however that there was nothing to say in reply; in effect he had (and perhaps was) compromised. Once he had intervened on Blent's side, however good the reasons might be, he must accept the full extent of his commitment, in silence. If his motives were misinterpreted, well, that was all there was to it, they would be misinterpreted.

"Never mind," he said to Da Silva, in deep disgust, "you don't understand, but never mind," and turned away defeated from a grin which seemed to him the height of insolence.

Just then, fortunately, the President rescued him

from being routed, and made an excuse for his leaving this disagreeable situation.

"Charles," he exclaimed, "how could I have missed you? Have you been here long?" And he steered Charles toward the hall, collecting and introducing the Senator and Mr. Sayre on the way. The four of them retired to President Nagel's study and shut the door.

"The Senator and Mr. Sayre," said the President to Charles, "have an interest in the matter we discussed this noon. I have briefed them on the position and said they might hear what you had to say. Of course, gentlemen—" his glance included all of them— "it's understood that this is confidential."

Charles looked closely at Herman Sayre, a powerfully built, bald man of fifty-odd, with white eyebrows and a heavy, rather dull expression on a face which might be thought pallid and flabby save for a certain haughtiness of expression and sullen imperiousness in and about the eyes; these returned his stare in a manner too cold to be thought of as arrogance, and in this glance alone Charles found some possible resemblance to Lily; at least he considered that she could probably look at one like that.

Does he realize that he is looking at his future son-in-law? This as yet absurd thought appeared to Charles to sum up also the secrecy of his position in the other question, the one they were here to discuss. For reasons he was just now unable to fathom, the connection was a disagreeable one.

"Young man," said Senator Stamp, "I hear that you failed this boy Blent in your course, is that right?"

The senator's voice was deep and kindly and terrifying; Charles already imagined a congressional investigation.

"Yes, sir, I did."

"I can understand how that must have been a disagreeable duty for you to perform," the Senator continued, "but you went ahead and performed it anyhow. We all sometimes must do things we'd rather not, and I want you to know, young man, that no blame attaches to you for it."

Charles wondered if he ought to say thank you.

"I am further given to understand," said the Senator, "that when Dr. Nagel explained the effect of that failure on the policy level, when he filled you in on, so to say, the broad picture—you were humane enough, reasonable enough, generous enough, to say that you would reconsider your decision."

"I said I would see Mr. Blent, yes," said Charles quietly and in a slight huff.

"Now, Senator," Dr. Nagel interrupted nervously as the old gentleman seemed about to go off again. "Perhaps it would be better if Mr. Osman presented the story as he sees it."

"I was only about to say," the Senator imperturbably resumed, "that I honor a man who is willing to think twice, and a man who moves with the situation."

"Anyhow, I gather the boy can play," said Herman Sayre.

"It turns out," Charles said, with a glance at the President, "that it's not up to me whether he can play or not. So far as I'm concerned, he can play—and once

116

I've said that," he added indignantly, "my ethical position doesn't matter to anyone, not even to me."

"Oh, now, I wouldn't say that," the Senator said.

"I have reasons of my own," Charles insisted, "and I think they're good reasons, and they are not your reasons, sir." This statement, he felt at once, was foolish and could lead into impossible embarrassment. He swung quickly to the President.

"You handled this business as you saw fit," he said, "and I've no doubt you had your reasons too; everyone has reasons. But you'll allow that from where I stand you showed mighty poor judgment."

"Charles, I wasn't keeping anything secret from you. There was no reason why you couldn't have known—"

"Except that I didn't know."

The President withdrew into his dignity.

"It was not my responsibility to keep you informed," he said. "An impartial observer might even suggest, Charles, that what another faculty member did in this matter was not relevant to your decision—was not your business, if you want it put more strongly."

"That's fine," Charles proclaimed at large, "that is just fine. But you let me make my decision, which very rapidly became Solomon's business after that, didn't it? So I'm made out to be a scab and company spy, my colleague on the faculty is subjected to treatment that amounts morally speaking to coercion, the coercion doesn't work—lo and behold, you're back where you were this morning."

"You surely don't mean you've changed your mind about Blent—again?" This incredulous question from the President, which could appear to Charles only as absurd, brought him to a stop.

"No," he said wearily after a moment. "For the reasons I spoke of, and which I won't discuss under any circumstances, I said that the student could compete in this football game, for all of me—that he ought to, in fact. And I am heartily sick of the whole question of Blent, and would like never to hear of it again. I'm talking about another question, which has to do with playing one faculty member off against the other. Naturally I spoke to Solomon and apologized." Charles glared around to see if anyone were going to dispute his right to do this. "Naturally he didn't accept the apology. How could he?"

"The technicalities of it don't interest me," said Mr. Sayre heavily. "Ordinarily, as you know, Harmon, I don't interfere in the running of this place one little bit. But this is so trivial, and it's my personal request— I promised my daughter I'd see to it that the boy friend got in the game. I don't see why a little thing like that should cause so much fuss."

"As I explained to you, Herman," the President said, "Mr. Solomon had a perfect right to do what he did. If he chooses to exercise that right against all persuasion, there is simply nothing I can do about it. I think, of course, that he's being unreasonable—"

"There's no room for unreasonable men in this College," said Mr. Sayre. "Let him think about that."

"Now, Herman, you know that one doesn't just up and fire a college teacher like that. Especially not for doing his job."

"Doesn't one? Seems a poor way to run a business."

"A college is not a business."

"So I gather."

The silence of stalemate settled down; everyone was angry except the Senator, who presently spoke.

"I can tell you right now," he said, "that I wish I hadn't got myself involved in all this. But I've got the boy's mother and dad downtown right now, in the hotel —in separate rooms; I understand they don't live together any more—and it's going to look mighty silly if they're sitting out on the fifty-yard line tomorrow and he don't play. Maybe, now, maybe if I sent his parents to see this Mr. Solomon, play on his heart strings—"

"I think not, Josie," said the President.

"Well, then, what about Professor Osman here? Young man, you speak of having reasons why Blent should play. Now I never pry into confidences. I respect your silence there. But is there any way you could use those reasons to convince your colleague, on personal grounds maybe?"

"At the same time you'd be setting yourself straight with him," said Dr. Nagel.

Charles wondered what would happen if he simply said that Raymond Blent had been bribed to throw the game. Most likely he would not be believed, inasmuch as such things did not really happen; even to himself, at this moment, the idea seemed improbable, and his hand went nervously to his wallet, which was puffed out with all those twenty-dollar bills.

"I don't think that would do any good, Senator," he said, and could not resist adding, "Besides, another faculty member's decision in this matter is not my business."

"Charles, if I was out of line on that I apologize," President Nagel said. "I take it back. I know you're sick of this whole business, too; so am I. But would you consider now taking this one further step for us? It's too bad the whole thing has built up so, but as we're in it this far I think we should push on to the finish, if it can be arrived at legally at all."

"A little more of this tricky ball-handling," said Herman Sayre, "and you'll lose the ball. Isn't this Solomon fellow the one who told our loyalty committee to go to hell? What about that?"

"Now, Herman, I should rather not bring that into it," the President said. "That is quite another matter, and I assure you that Solomon's background is still being inquired into—"

"A very serious business, that," observed the Senator. "Football is, after all, an American sport, it is a precious part of our national character, and if any shadow of subversion—"

"Time for a straight power play," Mr. Sayre said. "Straight up the middle. I think I'll go have a talk with Professor Solomon myself. If you won't set him straight, Harmon, that's one thing, but he is going to be set straight one way or the other."

"I agree," the Senator said. "Where does the man live?"

Charles looked at the President to see how he would handle this. For clearly it was up to the President of the College, at this moment, to interfere decisively. The other two were already on their feet.

"Gentlemen, this is not the way," said Dr. Nagel.

"I think you're insane, the pair of you," said Charles abruptly and somewhat to his own surprise. This opening had at least the effect of drawing their attention. They looked at him with a blankness somewhat sinister, as if he had said something (he probably had) which no civilized person could understand, let alone countenance.

"What is coming off tomorrow," Charles went ahead, "is a football game. That is very nice. I enjoy football games. Fine, clean American sport, best amateur tradition, lots of color, great for building character, gets everyone out in the fresh air once a week. That's all splendid. The fine young men who play it are largely hired men, but they are not paid enough to be called professionals. The game presents an image of war; it has a symbolic meaning, a value of that sort, and now and then someone breaks his neck at it, so it also has an element of reality.

"But how do you get from here to there? How do you arrive at power plays straight up the middle, at going off to threaten a teacher, blacken his reputation, perhaps take his job away? He hasn't even tried to prevent the game from being played, has he?"

Mr. Sayre stared at Charles and made a noise which sounded plainly like "Grrr."

"Young man," said Senator Stamp.

"I am not a young man," Charles said, "and if any of

you wishes to pull his rank on me I will resign instantly from this musical comedy institution of learning, remarking as I depart upon the fraudulence of its pretensions to intellectual and other respectability. Meanwhile, I will take advantage of the moment to say that you two gentlemen are making a bad mistake, and that if the President of this College does not resent your proposals, I do. If you go through with this extremely odd scheme of yours to put pressure on a colleague, I shall publish the fact in its full immoral absurdity."

Academic anger has a curious effect; people once subjected to it, in boyhood, get over the experience with difficulty or not at all. Both the Senator and Mr. Sayre were helplessly impressed, for the moment; as for President Nagel, he struggled with ambiguous fears. The victory, though, as Charles knew in the very moment of it, was empty.

"Moreover," he said more quietly, "circumstances condemn me to being partly on your side. This does not in the least alter the fact that I consider your behavior, both of you gentlemen, to be that of a pair of aged undergraduates whose unseemly view of sport would look more appropriate among the Hitler Youth—"

"Charles!" cried Dr. Nagel in a kind of stern hysteria. The others merely looked.

"When I have had my dinner," Charles said very deliberately, "I will talk to Mr. Solomon myself. For the reasons I have refused to tell you of, I think Mr. Blent should be permitted to play. But I will not go further with a colleague than reasonable persuasion.

And for your part, gentlemen, you will do nothing until you hear from me later this evening. And nothing after that. If I fail, you fail, we all do for that matter. Can I reach you here after, say, ten?"

There followed a prolonged silence, in which Charles felt his words echo foolishly in his own ears. Then Mr. Sayre spoke.

"I'll take you up on that, Osman," he said. "And it's good to know your mind, too. But I don't have to have a man love me, if he gets done what I want done."

"You see, young man," Senator Stamp said patiently, "for all your ill-temper, which I forgive, you're doing just what I asked you to do a few minutes ago. I'll be glad to leave the work to you, and we'll expect your call here after ten, or leave a number where you can reach us."

Those two gentlemen now left the President's study, while Charles and Dr. Nagel faced one another.

"I'll see you to the door," Nagel said; he seemed to be trembling. "No, not back through all those people. Come this way." He guided Charles by the arm down the hall and through the kitchen. Two students in white coats looked up curiously; one of them was Lou da Silva, who smiled darkly.

"Do what you can with Solomon," Dr. Nagel said, almost whispering. "But you should never have said those things."

"Someone had to say them," Charles replied sharply. "You would have let them get away with it."

"Not so loud, please, Charles. I would have found

123

some way to talk them out of it, surely you know that? But *insane—aged undergraduates—Hitler Youth—* Charles, that was too much."

As the President hastily opened the kitchen door Charles threw off the guiding hand under his elbow.

"My coat and hat," he said firmly. "And I'll leave by the front door, if you don't mind."

So back they went through the hall. Just as he was leaving Charles said, "Your only trouble is that your allegiance is divided."

Dr. Nagel smiled a sadly Machiavellian smile.

"Between what and what?" he asked.

"Between right and wrong," Charles replied, and went down the steps to the driveway without looking back.

2

What Charles meant by declaring to himself the intention of marrying Lily Sayre was not altogether clear to him when he left the President's house and went to call for her. In one way it was a most simple-minded decision, scarcely having to do with the girl herself at all; he was not even in love with her, though delighted and charmed with her qualities—of which he could have made a catalogue without ever actually recalling what she looked like. The decision in this respect represented feelings whose very existence in him was as yet, perhaps, theoretical; as though this girl, or at least his idea of this girl, crystallized in him vague tendencies toward the renewed possession of life, toward the assertion of oneself in the field of reality; tendencies which,

124

for all that they are regarded as normal, had suffered the severe shock of defeat in Charles upon the death of his wife some years before, and gone as it were into hiding. Involved sentiments of guilt and inadmissible relief had made it seem certain to him all this time that he should not try a second venture of the sort; now, in a day, that certainty had dissolved, or been replaced by an equal and opposite force.

As he walked along to the fraternity house, having had to leave his car at some distance, Charles felt an elated nervousness increased by his indignation over what had just taken place, in which he thought he had acquitted himself well. For possible reprisals he had a fine scorn, whose edge was only slightly blunted by his sense that he could afford such an attitude, that "the other side," that of administration and authority, could not risk attacking either himself or his position without appearing both foolish and dishonest; even should such an attack be made, he was satisfied nevertheless to have defended both principle and humanity at once—there were other colleges in the country. Just now, in fact, he felt a clear, balanced mastery of "the situation" both in its secret and its public aspects, extending to the perfect assurance of his ability to convince Leon Solomon, later on, of the rights of the matter, granted (what he hoped to hint at without disclosing) the special circumstances involved.

Was he not, finally, the man of sense, *honnête homme*, and, as illustrating that ideal, ideally fitted to courting the lady who had expressed it? Charles was pleased to view himself in the role of Count Mosca, bowing, smiling, concealing; and as there existed no portrait of that great gentleman of fiction, his image in Charles's mind assumed the thin, intelligent, rather dour features of Machiavelli.

Arrived at Alpha Sigma under the influence of this vision, Charles kept himself aloof from the party and waited in the hall while someone was sent to find Miss Sayre. Even so, inscrutable and enigmatic as he thought he appeared, he was joked at rudely by two or three passing undergraduates, students of his, who, being somewhat drunk, took the occasion to express a licensed familiarity which they valued, perhaps, for its supposed power of breeding contempt. Charles began to feel ill-at-ease, and remembered how miserable it used to be, in his own college days, standing in the entry of dormitory or sorority while someone went to fetch his date whose appearance from upstairs was anticipated by bursts of laughter and remarks, shouted in whispers, about "men."

She wore a black evening gown very severely cut and unadorned, but leaving naked her shoulders and arms. Around her neck lay a heavy, flat chain of gold. These contrasts particularly of texture, the flesh, the funereal cloth, the solidity and hardness of the metal, produced an impression very striking of aristocracy and slavery together. The expensive perfection of the object of desire provoked in the beholder, as it was meant to do, destructive longings to seize the chain, strip off the gown, dishevel the hair. This, Charles hopelessly thought, was what he had assumed he would marry if he cared to; and perhaps, from her smile and glance, she was quite aware of that intention, or for her part assumed it in any man she faced, as the result of what she had called erotic snob appeal.

A young man in dinner clothes, with whom Charles was not acquainted, got her cloak and, in helping her on with it, whispered something in her ear; Lily leaned her head back against his shoulder and laughed.

"I'm not lost forever," she said. "I'll be back." Then she took Charles's arm and they left. She was also, he thought, a little bit drunk.

"We'll take my car," she said before he could explain where his was; the Bugatti stood, in fact, just at the front door. They got in, and had their first quarrel at once.

"That dreary soup-kitchen?" was Lily's response to the news that they were going to the Aaron Burr for dinner. "Where every Rover Boy in the place will be taking his date and his parents too?"

"Still," Charles said, "there's a reason."

"I know a dark and dirty little *boîte* out on route 10," she said. "It's only twenty miles or so. We'll go there." And she started the car.

"We can't," he replied. "I've made a reservation already."

"Life needn't stop for a reservation."

"I don't want to talk about it till we get there," Charles said, "but please accept it that I have a good reason for wanting to go there instead of somewhere else."

"If you insist," she said, moving the car from the curb with some sullen violence.

Whether drunk or not, she drove furiously but with admirable concentration. The brief trip to town, a matter of only a few miles, frightened Charles a number of times, and to his later reflection it appeared that this drive somehow had been the turning point in the entire situation, the place at which matters began to go beyond his control, and that this change revealed itself in the fact that he was being driven by another, an experience which he had never cared for anyhow. In the same way, this drive made the difference between deciding to marry this girl, and falling in love with her.

The car was open, and so close to the ground that one had a new sense of being related to the road, which made a noise as loud as the cold wind. They did not speak at all during this time, and only as they got out of the car in the parking lot of the Aaron Burr did Lily say, "I'm sorry if I was a bother about coming here. Forgive?"

"Don't think of it." They smiled at one another and went in. It seemed an immediate justification of Lily's views, however, when on the way to their table they were stopped by young Mr. Barber, who rose from his place, napkin clutched in hand and mouth full of food, and stood, smiling and swallowing, in the aisle.

"Dr. Osman, delighted," he said when he could. "Hello, Lily. Sir, I'd like you to meet my folks—Mother and Dad, this is Dr. Osman, one of the members of our faculty. And this is my fiancée, Geraldine Pearl."

Greetings were awkwardly exchanged. Mr. Barber's father was a small, wizened man; it looked as though he had exhausted himself in producing so prosperous an expansion as his son, whose fiancée, in Charles's opinion, was agreeably commonplace in appearance and significantly resembled the mother. The young Mr. Barber now drew Charles ponderously aside, leaving Lily to wait under the admiration of the entire roomful of people.

"I can't tell you, sir, how relieved and gratified I am," Barber said in a low voice, "that our little contretemps this morning has come out so happily. And I do want to say, sir, that if you gave in I quite understand it was not in deference to my wishes, but in the name of something bigger than either of us. It was a generous thing to do, Dr. Osman, and I hope you've forgiven me if I said anything this morning that offended you."

"Mr. Barber," Charles began, but at the sight of that open and meaningless face before him had to smile forgivingly. "Mr. Barber, how good it must be to be you."

The face clearly either could not or did not care to interpret this remark; it smiled back at him.

"Fine girl, Lily," Mr. Barber said. "I didn't know you two were acquainted."

"I hope you've no objection," Charles said. "But we really must get on, now."

He turned back and took Lily's arm; as they moved away they heard Barber's mother saying, "Is that usual? Do teachers—?"

"Hush, Mom," said young Mr. Barber, quite audibly. "There is nothing wrong with it, is there? In fact, I believe she is his niece."

Charles blushed.

"Don't be embarrassed, Uncle," said Lily as they sat

down at table. "By the way, I hope it is proper for me to use your first name on this special occasion?"

"I hope you will," he said.

"Charles, then. A nice name. Charles. It isn't terrible, is it, our being *seen* together? I mean, you're not worried about your wife knowing?"

"I'm not married," he said. "That is, my wife is dead."

"I'm sorry."

"It was a long time ago."

"Now, Charles, order me something to drink, bourbon on the rocks will do, and tell me just why we had to come here."

"It's rather a delicate business," he said, looking into her eyes. "I don't know how much it's right for me to tell you. Though I want very much to be able to talk the whole thing over with you especially. A good deal has happened since I saw you last."

Charles ordered drinks.

"Please ask Mr. Giardineri if he would join us for a few moments and a drink," he told the waiter, who replied that Mr. Giardineri was very busy just now, but he would see what could be done.

"The mystery deepens," said Lily.

"In the first place," he began, "if it is the first place—did you know, this morning, that your young man failed not only my course but another one besides, Mr. Solomon's course in philosophy?"

"Yes," she replied, "I'm afraid I did."

"Why didn't you tell me?"

"Ah, that was unfair, wasn't it?"

"I thought so."

"But it was scarcely up to me to bring you two together, was it? I thought I had a better chance if I went at you one at a time. I called on Mr. Solomon just after lunch."

"And—?"

"And I got nowhere. You were both a credit to the teaching profession, men of principle, both of you; though he took a pleasure in it which you didn't. I don't think I could get along with Mr. Solomon."

"I've just had the experience of meeting your father," Charles said. "I don't think I could get along with him, either. Which is too bad," he added, meaning to say boldly "because I hope to marry you" but losing his nerve instead.

"Why is it too bad?" asked Lily, but just then the waiter came with the drinks and the news that Mr. Giardineri would come over in a few minutes.

"I can see you, in a way, as responsible for a good deal in this business," he said, "which may be nastier than you know, as well as more complicated. Your father seems to care for you deeply."

"His wife is dead, too," she answered. "Daddy thinks he does everything for my happiness."

"So when you failed with me, and failed with Solomon," Charles said, "you went straight along to the old man, isn't that so?"

"Yes, certainly. What else could I do?"

"Is it that important to you? I mean, couldn't you simply have let it go?"

"It is that important, yes. It is something I want done."

131

"Well, it produced a certain effect," said Charles heavily. "Your daddy, aided and abetted by Senator Stamp, has terrorized the President of the College and was practically on his way to bludgeon Mr. Solomon into submission. I stopped him."

"Why?"

"Why? My dear Lily, because, don't you see, one doesn't do that to people. No matter how much one wants a thing."

"But he didn't bludgeon you?"

"No," Charles said. "But my stand in the matter wasn't exactly heroic. He didn't need to bludgeon me, because I was already on his side, unfortunately. And that, obscure as it seems, is why we're here. Let me put it this way, Lily—on account of certain things that have happened today, I am forced to allow that Ray should be in the game tomorrow. I resent very much being placed in that position, but I'll go further and say that so far as I'm concerned he must play. He is a little less simple, your boy, than you believe."

"Yes," she said, "I'm afraid you're right. I may have misjudged him somewhere."

"Now what do you mean by that?"

"Never mind. Go on with your tale of woe."

"That's the point," Charles said. "I don't know if I ought to tell you straight out. It is a confidence. Yet it is one I hate to bear all alone, and I think if anyone knows you ought to be the one, because—I'll just say this for the moment—he deceived you about his reasons for going ineligible."

"Oh—you think that?"

Mr. Giardineri now came up and pulled out a chair but did not sit down. Instead he stood leaning on the chair-back, and frowning.

"I thought you'd be alone, Professor," he said.

"Well, I'm not," said Charles, and introduced Lily. "Please sit down, and stop looking so worried," he told Giardineri. "What I want you to do ought not to be difficult, and there's no reason for you to get into any trouble."

"Who needs a reason?" Giardineri said gloomily, but sat down nevertheless.

"Mr. Giardineri told me at lunch today," Charles said to Lily, "that tomorrow's game is fixed, he didn't say how."

"I never said that, Dr. Osman," said Giardineri.

"That's what I took it you had to mean, though," Charles replied. "Of course I wanted to think it was either a joke or an exaggeration, but later on in the afternoon I learned something which forced me to believe this statement was literally true. Someone has been bribed."

"The guy we were talking about at lunch," Giardineri promptly said.

"The object at present," Charles returned, "is to keep this business impersonal. Names needn't come into it. I'm not admitting it is the person you think," he added. "And for various reasons—of which a certain want of evidence is the least, by the way—I do not want to turn the matter over to the authorities for investigation.

"But there has been, let us say, a change. The party of the first part wishes to clear himself of his dishonest behavior—and *will do so, at any cost.* This may be sad news for your friends, Mr. Giardineri, but I take it they would rather know than not know; it might be wise for them to hedge those bets. In any case, I am empowered to return the advance payment to the proper person or persons. Now, do you think you could convey that information to the place where it ought to go?"

Mr. Giardineri frowned mightily at this.

"If it ever got out, Doc," he said, "there could be big trouble."

"It need not *get out*," Charles said. "I don't like it that way, I would prefer to blow the whole business up, but I can't. If we do it this way, no names have to come into it at all. I merely want you to arrange a meeting for me with one or more of the persons responsible; I'll do the rest. This meeting can either be right now, if the people are handy, or a good deal later tonight."

"Oh, it couldn't be now," the other man said earnestly. "They don't come running when I call, those guys. I don't really know them, you know. I just heard some things on the side."

"Will you try?"

"I'll have to make a few phone calls, Professor. It may take a while. And while we're at it, another thing. They're not going to meet you in this club. It'll have to be somewhere else."

"Wherever you like," Charles said. "And thanks. Now will you have a drink with us? I'm sorry I didn't ask before, but I wanted this thing settled."

"No, I'm busy now," Giardineri said, getting up and bowing slightly to the girl. "Nice to meet you, Miss."

134

"Have a brandy with us after you make the phone calls," said Charles.

"We'll see, we'll see." Mr. Giardineri moved off, looking rather burdened.

"So now you know," said Charles to Lily, who did not look as shocked as he thought she should.

"Dear Charles, you are a solemn person," she said, laughing. "Let's have another drink."

"I'm glad you're able to see it as funny," he said grudgingly, but signaled to the waiter as requested.

"It is, terribly funny. Your hemming and hawing and hinting—why wouldn't you tell me directly?"

Charles thought that perhaps the time now had come to be direct.

"I thought it a mean thing to have to say about anyone," he said, "but especially about your friend, since I'm in competition with him. I'd like to marry you."

Her eyebrows went up, and her mouth formed an O of surprise; in all which Charles detected no surprise whatever.

"All's fair, no doubt," she said, "but you took good care that I should know anyhow—you might as well have been more straightforward about it." The drinks arrived, Lily raised her glass: "Success to your schemes, Charles," she said, and drank.

"Well, then, you see that it wasn't for you, after all, that he failed those exams and kicked up all this stupid row."

"But it was, dear, it was. You see, *I knew*—oh, not this morning, when I spoke to you, no. What I told you then was what I believed. But this evening—after he saw you, and confessed, it seems confession made him feel so much better that he decided to try another dose. He got away from training table—the team's confined to the field house tonight, you know, except for that bonfire ceremony—and came to the party for a few minutes. He got me off in an alcove—on a window seat with a radiator under it, it was stifling—and gave me the entire story, together with, I must say, the most abject admiration for you. Whatever he had done, or been about to do, moreover, would have been for me, and now he wanted me to know it. We would have quit college and got married next week, all on his two thousand dollars. . . . Then he apologized for not being able to go through with it, and asked if I'd marry him anyhow."

"That is simple damn opportunism," said Charles, feeling both hurt and foolish. "He just wants to have the best of both ways."

"You can't blame anyone for that, can you?" she asked. "I was touched. How couldn't I have been? Nobody has ever become a criminal for my sake before, even if Ray didn't quite go the whole distance."

"And are you going to marry him?"

"Ah, as to that—" She shrugged her shoulders. "Charles, I couldn't know that you were going to complicate things. Look." She turned down the edge of her dress slightly.

"I took back his pin. My poor pathetic corrupted hero has his claim on me again," she said. "I promised to wear it at least till after the game."

"In secret?" Charles tried to smile.

"Yes—so now I have betrayed a confidence to you in exchange for yours, even if yours really wasn't one. In secret, because the lodge brothers had been after me, as I told you, on just that point, and I refused to let them believe they had changed my mind."

"And after the game—what?"

"Charles, you mustn't be so glum. Do get us another drink."

"Don't you think we should order supper?"

"One more, and then. All right?"

"Very well."

"As to what happens after the game—I consented to having a 'serious talk' about 'our' future. Though what future there is in it I can't quite see. Still, I owe him that—and the pin—because he does love me, I think, and there's not so much of that in the world that one can afford to be ungrateful."

"And the man of sense?" Charles had been trying for some minutes to keep these words back, but out they came at last.

"Ah, Charles, you do fit the description better than poor Raymond," she said with a smile. "Did you take it as an invitation, then, when I talked that way this morning? I didn't mean it so. Or, I guess, maybe I did, a little, since I can remember liking you a great deal at once. Why did you decide you wanted to marry me?"

"I thought about you a lot today," he began, feeling painfully that to be honest just here was at once necessary and foolish, "and I have to admit reaching the decision in a not very romantic way. I thought you were the right person for me. Then, when I saw you again, I fell in love with you—in the car, on the way here. I don't know how such things happen but they happen."

"Oh, they do," she said very gravely.

"I hope I don't embarrass you," he said. "We're not exactly of an age, either, are we?"

"But I'm very pleased, Charles, and flattered," Lily said. "There's something you've left out, though."

"What's that?"

"You haven't asked if I return your feeling."

"It strikes me," he replied, "that after what you've told me I have no right to ask that."

"My dear professor," said Lily, "you shouldn't be so desperately honest—it makes the rest of us look bad."

"Aren't you?" he asked.

After considering for a moment, she replied: "No, I don't think so."

Charles insisted then that they order dinner. But presently he came back to the subject.

"I have to talk of this," he said, "even if it comes under the heading of gossip about my rival. But I must know what you think. I was—I still am—horrified at what Blent did, or set out to do. I've always thought I had a fair understanding of the world, and why people did what they did, but this thing is somehow out of my range.

"Oh, theoretically, I suppose, I can understand such an action. If I am told, generally speaking, that this is a world in which people take bribes, I don't have any difficulty consenting; it is, that's all there is to it. But that this boy Blent did it—that's another matter. Not

138

that I thought about his character much—I never had occasion to—but just in passing I'd always assumed something fine in him, and something—on no particular evidence at all, mind you—beyond and better than the stereotype of the great athlete. And now he has done this—this stupid and vicious act, which is no less stupid and vicious for his attempts to recover himself.

"Well, that's my problem—believing it, knowing how one ought to respond to it. But what I want, Lily, is to know your view of it. What do you honestly think of him now?"

"This *is* a frontal assault," she said, but then looked at him seriously for a time before replying.

"I was touched and amused," she said at last, "nothing but that. I wanted to laugh at him for being so serious, and I couldn't, because he was being so serious. But while I laughed I would have kissed him because he had done it for me. Since I couldn't do the one, I wouldn't do the other, so I did nothing."

"I see," Charles said. "It didn't shake you anywhere, then?"

"Ray has never seen two thousand dollars," Lily said, "and I don't know which was more pathetic—the gallant gesture or the idea that two thousand was enough." She looked at Charles steadily. "I'd damn well have married him if he'd gone through with it," she said, "but I couldn't tell him that, could I—after he'd failed?"

"You're trying to shock me," Charles said. "Don't you care about the rights of things at all?"

"I'm only being honest about what I felt," she replied,

"as you wanted me to be. As for the rights of things, my dear and respected teacher, maybe I know as much about that as you do. I've had the advantage, don't forget, of seeing the world from the factory where the rights of things are run up as required. If you really want to know, I think that the idea of their oh-so-serious football game being a fake is a perfectly uproarious idea. All the banners and the bands, and those determined young chins, the dignified elders watching with grave approval, the drunken elders, with tears in their eyes, carried back to the days of their ideally reconstructed adolescence, all the talk about courage and character—it's the perfect celebration of fake to begin with. Why shouldn't it have, for once, a perfectly real fake at the center of it all? You needn't look pained and bewildered at me, Charles, either. I suspect you really believe the same thing."

"I may do," he replied. "I may do, in some very general way. But when you get over that, personal honesty remains, not as a principle or a conscious belief, perhaps, but simply as personal honesty: one does not do such things oneself, and that's all there is to it."

"Personal toilet-training," said Lily.

"Please," Charles said, "don't exercise that undergraduate smartness on me."

"As you wish, darling," she replied, "but you wanted to know what I thought, and I've told you. Would you rather I'd lied and said it was all too horrid for words? But I don't believe it's too horrid for words. I simply see it as one more sign of the big, permanent falsehood one has to deal with everywhere—how do you think my father got where he is?"

"That's a very old argument," Charles said, "but civilization goes on anyhow."

"And what is civilization," she demanded, "if it's not my daddy? Do you think it's you?"

"Now look," he said patiently. "Here's the proof. Even Blent, who got us into this stupid quarrel, even he knows that one thing is right and another is wrong. He simply feels it's so. He told me, this will show the seriousness of it; he told me that if they lose tomorrow he'll kill himself. Of course I don't think he will—that's kind of boyish, though heroically boyish—but it suggests, doesn't it, what all this means to him?"

"But if he doesn't," Lily said with a cold expression on her face, "and he won't, then it is neither heroic nor serious, but only boyish, isn't it?"

"You're entitled to your own belief, of course," Charles muttered, and she laughed.

"Don't fight with me, Charles. I didn't mean it that way. You want to win the argument and be right, but I don't want to win the argument and be right, I only want to do as I please."

"A large order," he said grimly, but then had to smile.

"Tell me," he said a moment afterward, "have I merely lost touch with the way things are? Would you say that your whole generation, the one I supposedly teach, thinks as you do?"

"Pedant," she said, rather tenderly. "I doubt it. They're mostly like you, I suppose, but less intelligent.

141

More like Ray, perhaps, serious, idealistic, well-meaning, and finally dishonest with themselves. Maybe you and Ray are not so different after all," she added.

"And you?"

"I am the way I am." Lily seemed to stop here on the edge of some other statement, then said, "I'm neither very happy nor very nice."

"Don't think that," Charles said earnestly, taking her hand. "Everyone is sort of miserable when he's young, you know."

"Ah, nuncle," she said, removing her hand, and then, with a sudden lightness oddly inappropriate to the subject, "tell me something about your wife—what was she like?"

"Well . . ." Charles hesitated. "She was—she was very nice," he said inadequately. "I didn't mean that as a deliberate contrast," he added. "But she wasn't happy, either."

"Oh?"

"She took her own life," he said quite suddenly. "So I guess it's fair to say she wasn't happy."

"Were you?"

"No," he said. "Perhaps we would not have stayed together in any event. But I never understood why she did it. I mean—it made me feel like a monster of some sort, and I don't really believe I am one. What did I do to her?"

"I can't answer that for you," Lily said.

"No, of course not—it is just that I haven't talked about it to anyone for a long time."

"Please don't, if it hurts you."

"No, no—anyhow," he added, and attempted to smile, "you ought to know, I suppose, about the risk you'd run in marrying me.

"She took sleeping pills, and she sometimes talked of suicide—which made me think according to the rules of *Readers' Digest* psychology, that there was no danger. But one day when I came home—it wasn't here, but at another school—the house was all silent, the windows were open and all the curtains blowing, it was a cold spring day and still very light out, and no one answered when I called.

"I made myself a drink and stood around nervously in the kitchen. 'She's left me, finally,' I thought—that was another thing she talked about a good deal. But then I began to feel more and more uneasy, until I was near sick with nervousness. I called her name a number of times, very loud—a ridiculous thing to do, supposing she had left—and then I climbed the stairs, and there she was in bed. She had dressed in a white silk nightgown, and was all prettied up with lipstick and perfume, and—I noticed this particularly—she had rearranged the pillows and moved into the center of the double bed. And the curtains were blowing in at the windows, as I said. It was all so peaceful, and rather Hollywood in style. I mean by that, not only that it was repulsive—that feeling came later—but in the first place that it was like a scene in a movie, so silent and remote, as if one weren't quite inside it oneself but observing it from a distance."

"What did you think?" Lily asked.

"There wasn't much to think—perhaps I didn't have

any thoughts for a while, I don't know. It's something I don't want to talk about," he added roughly.

"You wished for her death," said Lily simply.

"You're too young to know how such things are. You ought not to know. It was all—quite mixed, anyhow."

"I understand," she said.

"And then—then there was a good deal of civil commotion, with people to see and questions to answer, telegrams to send, arrangements to be made. Everyone," he added, "was most understanding."

"Except yourself?"

"Except myself, I guess."

"I'm sorry, Charles." She touched his hand. "Terrible thoughts. Don't think them any more."

Mr. Giardineri approached and consented to have a Benedictine.

"I fixed up something for you," he said in a conspiratorial voice. "But God help us all if you make a wrong move, sir. I'm trusting you further than I can see you by a long way."

"Don't worry," Charles said. "We're not in the jungle, you know. Nothing will happen."

"I wish I had your faith, Doc," said Giardineri. "Anyhow, you know Depot Street, that runs past the station, just where the buses turn around to come back?"

"Yes."

"Nick's Railroad Grill, on that corner. Between eleven and twelve. You ask the barman if you can talk to Max. That's all. He doesn't want to know your name, you don't want to know his name, and above all don't mention my name. You see," he added, "I didn't talk to the guy myself, only, you know, the friend of a friend of a friend. And it'd be better if the young lady didn't go down there with you. That's a rough neighborhood at night."

"Thanks very much," Charles said. Mr. Giardineri, for all his furtiveness, appeared pleased with himself.

"I wouldn't have done this for everybody, Professor Osman," he said, and waved to the waiter, to whom he added imperiously, "The liqueurs are on me, Jack." And so he left.

"I'm going, though," said Lily. "Imagine—criminal doings in our little community! Who would miss it?"

"Giardineri's quite right, though," said Charles. "It's no place for you to be."

"I've been thrown out of deeper underworlds than he knows anything about," she said, "or you either. You'll take me anyhow, or I shall follow with horn blowing and Tell All."

3

The bonfire blazed high, making in the darkness a cavern of uncertain light and long shadows. From the road above the practice fields, where Lily insisted on stopping the car, they saw the gathering of a crowd not as yet very large and quite disorganized; people seemed to be walking about rather aimlessly, though there was some singing, too, which could be heard spasmodically, as if some of the singers only intermittently thought it worth while to take part. It sounded, at this distance, like muttering more than music, and had a vaguely ominous feeling about it. In the space between the

145

crowd and the fire, a few people in white sweaters capered around, turned handsprings, or merely talked to each other, and two personages enormously mounted on stilts held between them a banner some twenty feet long, emblazoned with the name of the College. Cars were still being parked, though, and people were drifting in from the direction of the dormitories and fraternity houses. Now and then, some small area of the crowd would suddenly form itself into an order more compact than the rest, and thence came some rhythmic chant or cheer, in which could frequently be heard, like a strangled or hysterical bark, the word "Fight."

Lily leaned into Charles's arms and they kissed seriously. Some cars and a large bus drove by, and from the windows of these, close above, came a few cries of obscene admonition and abuse.

"That will be the team, in that bus," said Lily.

"Each to his own business and desires," Charles said, and they kissed again. It was very cold.

"Maybe you feel we should not be doing this," Charles said.

"If I did," she answered, "we wouldn't be doing it."

That bus had driven down on the field, and a large informal roaring began as the members of the football squad got out and paraded through the crowd to a wooden stand on one side of the bonfire. At the same time, from behind the stadium, the college band came marching and playing; fragmentary phrases of blaring and thumping bounced from the stadium wall; the cheers of the crowd, becoming somewhat more disciplined, began to break one after another like waves on a beach.

"I should go along now," said Charles unwillingly. "Solomon lives up this road just a little way. I can walk. Or you could drive me back to where I left my car."

"Stay with me for a few minutes. I'll take you to his house. After all, sir, I want to keep track of you so that you don't elude me later on."

"You ought not to go, Lily. It's not necessary."

"But it'll be fun. And you will protect me from harm."

"You're leaning on a broken reed," he said.

"I'll call for you in an hour or so."

"I do want to be with you, very much," said Charles. "But I think it's a damn-fool idea."

"Much the best sort," she assured him, and came to be kissed again. These kisses, in keeping with the situation, were rather cold though tender, but in spite of gloves, coat, hat, a certain agitation began to be apparent. Charles decisively broke off the engagement.

"This may be a little foolish of us," he said. "And not quite honest, either. I'm serious, Lily. I do love you, and I do want to marry you, are you clear about that?"

"Yes," in a small voice.

"Do you love me?"

She was silent for a minute before answering.

"You want to rely on me," she finally said, "and I'm not reliable."

"Do you?"

"Ah, I could say yes—" She sighed. "I take a pleasure in you, Charles."

"I quite understand," he said grumpily and with no grace; and he began making slow, demonstrative gestures toward getting out of the car.

"I shouldn't stop you," Lily said, "but I will. I'll say it, but you've been warned. You must just take me the way I am."

"Say it."

"I love you, Charles."

This statement, rather flatly given, left him if anything more disappointed than before.

"What about our hero down there?" He gestured toward the bonfire.

"I don't know," she said. "I just don't know."

"Will you take off that silly pin—now?"

"You must be more patient than that," said she. "I promised to wear it till after the game, and I must."

"I don't see that."

"As you said, personal honesty remains," she reminded him, "though Lord knows it comes in all shapes and sizes. I'm very attracted to you, Charles."

"This is a sad discussion," he said. "We're sitting out here like strays in a storm. Come to my apartment."

"Not now. You have to see Solomon, then we have to go down into the provincial underworld, remember?"

"We could forget it all."

"I won't, though. We'll simply sit here being friends for a few minutes more, till we are both thoroughly frozen, then I'll drive you along. Look—I think the head coach is about to administer the sacrament."

Through the microphone the thin, tinny voice came faintly and intermittently up to them, accented with electrical coughs, interrupted by bursts of cheering and applause. A light breeze had come up, in whose gusts the coach's words were by turns amplified and muted, as if they were written on a banner which folded and unfurled.

". . . make no promises . . . the true fighting spirit . . . heard the other day . . . said to the Jew . . . Begorra, said the Irishman . . . even the Pope himself . . . so in the same way, on the field tomorrow . . . nothing I can say that matters . . . remember, we will . . . I promise you that."

"Fight team fight" cried the crowd.

"And then they'll have a wienie roast and go home victorious," said Lily, who was more or less lying in Charles's arms.

"It makes me sad, this kind of thing," he said. "It always makes me sad."

"You don't get the real feel of it, maybe."

"I think it's because I do, or because there is real feeling to it. Because crowds are always serious, and menacing."

"This crowd?"

"Whenever people get together to convince themselves that life is more glorious than life is. Behind it all there lies terrible disappointment."

"Ah, now, they're only having fun."

"But they're not, and if they should ever realize it while they were still a crowd, instead of on the way home, when they become sad and lonely people again, you'd have the same sort of fun that goes into lynchings and pogroms—because these things need a certain reality somewhere at the heart of them, to be truly successful. For the real catharsis, they ought to burn a football player—a spare one, maybe."

"What a charming thought," she said. "And then eat him?"

"Of course. You know, when I was a boy and used to play with toy soldiers, we used to have battles, my friends and I. At least, the object was to have a battle; and we would divide up the forces, arrange them strategically inside and around the fort we built out of blocks —but just there reality left off, let us down, since whatever our toy soldiers would do for us they wouldn't move, so the battle itself was always something of a formality and a disappointment. We used to put it off as long as we could, by having parades, reviews, re-arrangements of the disposition of the troops, and so on, until we got tired of playing with the soldiers anyhow, or one of us lost his temper and knocked a whole division over with one hand. There's something of the same let-down built into this situation."

"Darling, you must have been a rather stolid, unimaginative child," said Lily. "And besides, the whole object of life is to make it more glorious and exciting than it is, even if you sometimes come down with a thud in the end."

The crowd around the fire was singing the "Alma Mater"—a dreary and funereal piece which rolled out over the dark space with a certain incoherent power.

"That thud," said Charles, "is the distant echo of the last spadeful of earth. Or not so distant, maybe," he added gloomily.

"To the virgins, to make much of time," said Lily. "Is that what you tell your classes, nuncle?"

"No," he said, "that is a secret revealed only to the elders of the tribe, after many degrees of initiation."

"A secret everybody knows, though."

"The secret, dear Lily, is not the knowing of it, but the learning to be frightened."

"Kiss me again," she said, and he did.

"The defense rests," she added, starting the car. Behind them as they drove away the crowd finished its lugubrious anthem and dissolved in loud, uncertain mutterings, as though the sense of the song had suddenly become unclear. The bonfire blazed higher than ever, sending up bright but vanishing sparks and filling the brilliant space in night with wavering shadows.

4

It was already nine-thirty when Charles climbed the steps of Solomon's front porch and rang the bell. He had no idea what he was going to say to the man, now the time had come, and it crossed his mind also that he ought to have phoned first to see if Solomon were at home, and to ask at least if he would receive a caller; that he had not done so seemed a mean indication that he had unconsciously as low a regard for the man as everyone else involved, and was willing, like them, to treat him as a convenience. Somehow it had never occurred to him that Solomon, like another, might have his own occasions elsewhere at this time. It was difficult to imagine him attending the pep rally, in whatever spirit; but he might quite simply have gone to the movies. Still, lights were on inside, and soon he heard steps. The curtain was drawn from the front door and a woman looked out at him with a severe expression before opening lock and bolt.

"Mrs. Solomon?" Charles introduced himself and said he had come to see her husband.

"Leon has gone to bed," she told him. "He is sick, and can't see anybody."

"It's rather important," Charles said. "I'm sorry."

"It's always important, isn't it?" But she let him into the front hall, where they stood for a moment looking at each other.

Mrs. Solomon was a small, thin woman, perhaps thirty years of age. Her face expressed a kind of desperate prettiness as though every line in it depended on nervous exasperation to be kept up together with the rest, as though in perpetual indecision whether to sag or explode. She wore a black sweater and skirt, and had in her hands a dish towel which she twisted tight.

"I'm sorry to hear he's ill," said Charles.

"Oh, it's nothing physical," she said with a scorn directed either at Charles or at the sick husband. "I suppose you've come about the great football crisis?"

"Yes, I'm afraid I have." His smile was not returned. "I know he won't want to see me, but if it is at all possible . . . Please tell him. Say I wouldn't have come if I didn't think something could be done, on his side as well as the other."

"I'll see," she said. "He must go through to the end,

that's something he doesn't want to realize." She turned toward the stairs, but stopped and came back.

"I'll take your coat and hat. Please wait in the living room. And if you want something to read meanwhile, try these."

From a salver on the hall table she picked up two envelopes and pushed them into his hands.

"Who wouldn't be sick?" she said furiously as she went upstairs.

Charles uncertainly opened the envelopes, which bore Solomon's name but had not gone through the mail. One, after some obscene epithets, said simply: "Go back to Russia where you belong." The other, with a horrifying joviality and reach of wit: "Dear Jew-boy, Reverse your field or be buried under it." Neither was signed. Charles shuddered and went into the living room as directed, the notes still in his hands.

This room expressed something of the sad domesticity of the underpaid instructor. It had begun, perhaps, with some design of elegance: a marble-top table on wrought-iron legs, a couple of very abstract chairs, of which the webbing had sagged, and a "modern" lamp with three great bell-heads which nodded musingly when Charles crossed the floor. Over the fireplace, which was a nest of cigarette butts, newspapers, and Kleenex, hung a blue Picasso reproduction flanked by half a dozen pieces of shelf paper covered with dots and blobs and scrawls of paint identified as being by Debbie, Joel and Ruth. Children's shoes and shirts and socks lay all about the floor, together with cars, airplanes, sprawled dolls and a battalion of black plastic soldiers lying as if sown in one sweep of the hand. On a faded green couch at the far end of the room a collection of newspapers had been wadded up to one side as though by someone about to lie down, and on the small table within reach were two dirty coffee cups and a full ash tray and a yellow-backed paper edition of Rousseau's *Confessions*. Next to the couch, on the floor, were the parts of a high fidelity phonograph in a nest of wires; the record on the turntable was of the "Three Blind Mice."

Charles rebuked himself seriously for finding all this funny or sad or repellent; there was no satisfactory response except that it was necessary, or the way things were these days. No doubt the classical ideal of the intellectual life, coming from the monasteries and throwing the women and children overboard first, had a hygienic austerity to it; but what that ideal had produced, century after century, was by no means exclusively the good the true and the beautiful either. At least it might be said in favor of the present arrangement that it expressed not so much an ideal as a mere necessity. Which might be a poor excuse, but there it was.

Charles straightened up on hearing a sound from the stairs, and was looking fixedly at the Picasso (a hunched old woman) when Leon Solomon came in. He was wearing white pajamas and a faded blue bathrobe, under the collar of which a towel was swathed about his neck, giving him a strangely athletic appearance. He shuffled across the floor to Charles, avoiding toys on the way, or nudging them to one side with the toe of a slipper. Not offering to shake hands, he nevertheless seemed more pleased at having company than Charles would have expected him to be. Charles had come prepared for antagonism if anything, but the look Solomon gave him was pathetic; behind the silver-rimmed glasses his eyes were red and wet.

"Let me get you a drink," he said.

"Oh, now," Charles said, "that's not necessary. I know I've no right to come walking in on you like this."

"We'll have a drink, anyhow." Charles followed him into the kitchen and watched while Solomon got out ice and fixed two strong highballs, which they took back into the living room. Mrs. Solomon had withdrawn to the front hall, where she could be heard walking up and down—a disturbing sound—during their conversation. Ready to run to his defense, thought Charles.

"Your wife showed me these," he said, holding up the two anonymous notes. "I think they are loathsome. I can understand how you would be upset—who wouldn't be?—but I hope you won't take expressions of that sort as serious or worth considering in the least."

"That's a great help," Solomon said with a touch of the expected acerbity. "I should pretend they never came?"

"There are always a few people like that around," Charles said, "who take out their private hatred and fear by any public means available. Whatever the disagreement," he added sternly, "this sort of trash doesn't represent anything substantial, it doesn't say anything about you, it doesn't say anything about the College either. You know that."

Solomon seemed about to say something, but what came out was a kind of whimpering noise.

"I feel I'm partly to blame," said Charles, "but maybe I can help straighten things out." How? he wondered.

Solomon had turned away and seemed to be busy polishing his glasses on the edge of his robe.

"You don't have any idea how it feels," he said, "to know that people hate you."

"I don't hate you," said Charles.

"Thank you." Even in this brief phrase the voice hesitated between sarcasm and sincerity. Solomon put the glasses back on and Charles saw that he was trembling.

"You've got a chill," he said.

"A chill in the metaphysics," said the other.

"Why don't you lie down on the couch, and we'll get a blanket—since probably you ought not to be out of bed?"

Solomon with a rebellious shaking of the head suffered himself to be led to the couch, where he stretched out with that pile of newspapers for a pillow. Mrs. Solomon, who clearly was listening to all this, at once brought in a blanket, tucked it round him, and retired again without a word to Charles, who heard her resume that pacing up and down the hall. He brought over a chair and sat down in its rather elastic net until his behind nearly touched the floor.

"I take it you haven't changed your mind about this thing?" he said. Mr. Solomon tried to smile.

"I've been saying no so many times today I can hardly remember what I'm saying it about. When I look back, it seems such a simple, trivial business, something about a football player, a rule, was it? He flunked my exam, something like that. Who cares?"

"You admit it's more serious than that now, don't you? Well, don't clown around, then. I sympathize," Charles added less sharply, "and I don't want to have to go over it all, any more than you do. But there are some things which have got to be said."

"Say, then, I'm listening." Solomon waved his hand languidly, then with an abrupt motion turned around and faced the wall.

"This first," said Charles, refusing to be disconcerted. "Without any more apologies, I think you are right and I am wrong. Your position was the only honest one, the only possible one, and I made a mistake trying to handle the thing in another way."

"Now he tells me."

"But on the other hand—"

"Aha! The other hand. The other hand is around my neck already."

"On the other hand," Charles continued, overriding all this, "I'm stuck with my mistake, just as much as you are stuck with your—wisdom, or morality, or whatever. I am not trying to defend my judgment to you, or to anyone else, but I want you to consider this: I know more about this situation than you do."

"Everybody knows more about everything than I do."

"Let me finish, then you can make remarks. I'm not defending myself, as I said, because I'd already made my mistake by the time I got to know this further thing which you don't know. What I want to convince you of is this: that in the light of this knowledge my stupidity, my dishonesty, if you want to call it that, is right, or at least necessary, while your otherwise impeccable behavior—"

"Is wrong or irrelevant—I know, don't tell me. On the one hand this, on the other hand that. Just what we teach our students, so they can grow up to be philosophers like us. Anybody could be Hegel if he had three hands."

"I know it sounds ridiculous," said Charles. "The way things are is often ridiculous." He looked gloomily around at the floor with its scattering of soldiers. Solomon said nothing.

"Blent failed your exam on purpose," he went on, "just as he did mine."

"That girl was at you, too, then? Do you believe it?"

"I happen to know it's true," Charles said, "but for other reasons."

"So does that make him a hero?"

"No, it doesn't. As a matter of fact, it's worse even than you think." Charles considered for a moment how far it was necessary to go, how much it was possible to tell. "What we've got," he said cautiously at last, "ought to be right up your street, a kind of problem in ethics. Listen, Leon, can I say something to you in confidence?"

"I'd much rather you didn't, but I suppose that makes no difference."

"You may not believe it," Charles said stiffly, "but I am trying to help you. Maybe I can't do much, but my coming here might save you from some of the nastier elements in the situation. Probably, though, you want to wallow in your inexpensive martyrdom instead. All right, the hell with you." With some effort he got himself out of the chair; one foot came down on a celluloid bomber, which crunched under his weight. "I'm sorry," he said, looking down at what he had done. Solomon turned around to see.

"Don't think of it," he said, "it'll mean a small increase in the defense budget. What do you want me to keep secret?"

"All I ask is that you won't get all political about what I'm going to tell you," Charles said. "I think you'll be tempted, from the little I know of you, to start raving about honesty and matters of principle . . . but I don't want you to do that. Whether the information changes your mind about anything or not is your own business, but I want you to promise you'll keep it absolutely to yourself. And that's partly for your own protection too," he added, "since I doubt anyone would believe you, in public anyhow—or me either, if it comes to that."

Solomon drew himself up on one elbow and looked thoughtfully at Charles.

"I promise," he said at last, "for your sake, Osman, since I can see you can't rest till you tell me. I bet I'll regret it, though."

"It's a splendid exercise for the soul, keeping things to yourself," said Charles. "I wish I could afford it myself, just now.

"Simply this, then. The boy took a bribe from some betting people, to throw the game. I wouldn't have thought it likely, either, but it happened by accident that there was some independent evidence—anyhow, I'm convinced it happened."

Leon Solomon grinned broadly, a rather wolfish expression.

"Wouldn't you know it?" he said happily. "Wouldn't you know it?"

"His conscience bothered him—perhaps as a result of his researches in modern ethical theory—" Charles could not forbear making this remark. "And as for various reasons I needn't go into he could not do anything directly about the deal, he decided to put himself out of action by becoming ineligible."

"How much was he getting?"

"Five hundred in advance," Charles replied, "and he would have got fifteen hundred more after the so-called contest."

"For two thousand fish I'd betray European thought since the Renaissance," said Solomon, "but I won't be asked. Always a bridesmaid, never a bride." He sighed. "This could blow the place wide open, couldn't it?"

"But it won't," Charles said sharply. "You've promised. It's the boy's whole future, think of that. And besides, there won't be any two thousand dollars. It so happens I think that part of it can be straightened out tonight. I can reach the other side, you see, and give back the advance. Then, if Blent can play, he's in the clear no matter which way the game goes. Now do you see why it's important that he be allowed to play?"

"He came to you and confessed all this, did he?"

"Yes, just after I spoke to you on the phone."

"With tears, eh?"

"Yes, with tears," Charles unwillingly allowed; Solomon seemed pleased at that.

"Why can't he just stay ineligible? That way, he's well out of it whatever happens."

"Because it's a matter of conscience," Charles said. "He feels, and I agree, that he must redeem himself somehow if it's at all possible. He can't just leave it there."

"A matter of conscience," said Solomon, and seemed to muse over this for a moment. Then he laughed. "You mean the entire creation is being reorganized just for him to be allowed to play," he said, "and it wouldn't look so sweet if he said he didn't really want to?"

"Of course that does enter into it," Charles admitted.

"A fine matter of conscience," said Solomon. "With a conscience like that, I could be king."

"Oh, relax," said Charles crossly. "What kind of impossible purity do you want, for Christ's sake? Didn't you ever make a mistake when you were young? The boy made a mistake, and the world could have fallen in on his head, but it hasn't; do you insist that it must?"

"So he confessed all this to you, and he cried, and he promised to make everything right and give back the ill-gotten gains?"

"Substantially, yes, that's what happened."

"And instead of calling for the cops you said, Go sin no more?"

"If you want to put it that way, yes, I did."

"I see." Solomon stared at Charles, who took it uncomfortably, and then said, getting to his feet, "Give me your glass."

They went into the kitchen again. Charles was aware once more of Mrs. Solomon standing in the shadows of the hall, not speaking but looking after them. Like a wild animal, he thought resentfully. Why doesn't she go sit down somewhere? Solomon paid her no heed.

"You are corrupted by Christianity," he said, standing by the sink and facing Charles. "Maybe we all are. But you more than me."

"What you say may be true," Charles began. "I don't keep up my religion, if it is my religion."

"Religion I'm not talking about," said Solomon. "It's deeper than religion. We live among the *goyyim* and we teach what they want taught, till we learn it ourselves. But we'll always be uneasy because what it finally means is, we teach what we don't believe."

"If it's any comfort, they don't believe it either," said Charles.

"But they do. There again it's not a matter of religious belief. Maybe you're right and it's not belief at all, only a kind of smugness that comes from being on the winning side. History, philosophy, poetry, all written by the winners—and we go along with it, you and I, making our cheap living by teaching the winners how good it is to think as they think and eat the bread and drink the wine."

Solomon handed Charles another highball.

"Here, drink the wine," he said, "and may it turn into a mystical football in your belly."

"I take it you mean I should have turned the boy in?" said Charles. "Reported the whole affair to Nagel at least, if not actually to the police?"

"It was your duty," Solomon said, "as what they call an officer of this College."

"You can say that, but it didn't happen to you, it happened to me. When it was put up to me squarely I didn't feel I could wreck the man's life."

"You don't know, though, what will wreck his life any more than you know what will save it. You took too much on yourself."

"Granting that's so," said Charles, "that one can't know, I mean—still, given any choice at all, the charitable way was the right one. Or so it seemed to me, and I still feel that way."

"Charity, sure, charity—you've learned to think the way *they* think. Let the weary and heavy-laden come to you, brother, and you'll fix it. Again, you took too much on yourself."

"Your idea of being a Jew, then, is that we go on demanding the pound of flesh over and over till time ends, that we never learn? And let me remind you that in this instance the injury hadn't been done to me, even."

"Hah! Whoever harms one of these little ones—that was what you were saying, wasn't it?"

"Nonsense. It simply seemed to me that I had no right to pass judgment on the boy. That may be originally a Christian view, but to me it is a matter quite simply of civilized behavior, no more."

"If you feel that way," said Solomon with a grim smile, "why didn't you turn him over to the Christers, and let them use some of their charity on him?"

Charles had nothing to say to this.

"Because why? Because they would have, as they say, turned him over to the secular arm and had him burned for the greater glory of American sport, that's why. So not only do you have to talk like Jesus because they think it's right, you also have to act like Jesus because they won't."

Again Charles said nothing.

"I'll tell you another thing—they would have been right. Hah! In a way, they're better Jews than you are, besides being better Christians. They would also have forgiven him, they'd have forgiven the hell out of him as soon as they had him safely in the pokey with the pound of flesh off his ass."

"Tell me this," said Charles after a prolonged silence. "Were you never forgiven for anything? Didn't you ever do anything out of line, or that you considered dishonest afterward? Even when you were young? Remember, twenty-one or so is not a very advanced age, and people are still sort of uncertain about the world even though they are said to have reached legal responsibility."

"You make mistakes, you suffer," said Solomon carelessly. "In my world you're not uncertain about that after the age when you begin to masturbate."

Charles hesitated for a moment on the feeling that he was doing a dreadful thing, then said, "What about the Communist party? That isn't something I enjoy bringing up, but since we're speaking in confidence I'll promise to include that—I want to bring the point home to you, that's all."

"If you know about that," Solomon said, "you know

how much I've been forgiven for it. A funny thing about that business, by the way. I wasn't, but I'm just as guilty as if I had been. Hah! You see, I thought I was. Half the way through college, I went around like a secret agent, heap big party member. Came the revolution I would stand everybody against the wall and give the word—especially traitors and intellectuals like you, brother," he added. "Weren't you in the party, by the way? You must have felt real left out of things, back in those days. The first girl I ever laid was a co-worker in a rally for the Lincoln Brigade."

"I just didn't take much of an interest in politics, I guess," said Charles.

"Anyhow," said Solomon, "I took it that was all over as soon as I graduated, you know, like singing in the glee club. The war was coming, and that was serious. Pacifism is all right in times of peace, and so forth. So when the time came I was going to be drafted I went around to what I had always thought was party head-quarters, or as good as—I wanted to resign, see?"

"And?"

"And there was nothing there. When I looked at the fine print on the back of my card, where it said Communist Party USA in big letters and the rest in small, I found it said that I belonged to the League for Individual Liberty, an organization which shared the purposes of—in large type—the Communist Party USA. The offices were empty, and there didn't seem to be anything left to resign from. I still have the card somewhere."

Charles considered that for a moment.

"Then I should think it would have been simple for you to clear yourself with that committee," he said, "and that would have been the end of it. Wouldn't that have been the easy way?"

"It was a matter of principle," said the other. "Those pious sons of bitches had no right to ask me what I did when. So I naturally refused to answer."

"You could have been forgiven, then," said Charles, "but you just refused, isn't that it? Pride, nothing but pride."

"What do I want with their forgiveness? Forgiveness for what? And from whom? Sweet weeping Jesus—if I may use the expression—I hadn't committed any crime. I am not a Communist, Osman, and as it turns out I wasn't." He added, after a pause, "They wouldn't have forgiven me anyhow, for even having thought I was. I'm not the sort of person that gets forgiven for things, and that's all there is to it."

Charles looked at his watch; it showed already well after ten.

"All right, all right," he said. "Beautiful are thy feet upon the mountain tops, you are a man of admirable character and inflexible will, like a jackass. I can't change your mind, I realize that, and furthermore I admit you're right, though I wish you could be right gracefully. The only thing I have left to say is personal. You believe I'm in the wrong, and I will admit again that if you go by principle I am—though the whole business still seems to me more complex than you allow, and I would do it the same way another time. But all I want to request is that you don't hate me, at least not

167

on political grounds. I'd like to be friends, no matter what happens. If that sounds a juvenile thing to say, put it down to the situation, which is in all conscience juvenile enough."

Solomon put his glass down on the drainboard and offered his hand, which Charles took.

"I'm not an easy person to be friends with," said Solomon. "I'm grateful for the offer, though. Sometimes it's hard not having anyone to talk to around here."

"I'm sorry for where this will leave Blent," said Charles, "though I suspect you haven't heard the last of that yet. But I've done what I could, and probably the kid will make out one way or another, like the rest of us. That's my last word on the subject, thank God. Only keep it quiet, what I told you."

"That was a promise," said Solomon gravely. Then he laughed, and added, "I'll do better than that—since you ask me as a friend, what can I refuse you? Let the boy play, for all I care, only it shouldn't be a matter of principle, right?"

"I assure you," Charles said, "that I had no idea of using friendship—"

"Always the perfect gent," said Leon. "But it's odd, isn't it, how one answers up to being used like a human being?"

There were steps in the hall. Mrs. Solomon came into the kitchen and stood facing the two of them.

"I've heard all of this I can stand," she cried furiously, and then, disregarding Charles, addressed herself solely to Leon.

"You go on as you please, like a great gentleman," she

said, "do this, do that, do the other, exactly as it comes into your head. But how do you imagine I feel? Who do you think has supported your stupid honesty for ten years, your arrogance, your ill-temper, your high principles and your hysterical fits? You get one smile from him—" she nodded her head sharply toward Charles— "and all that goes out the window. Oh, you won't change your views, not if they gave you the world in a tea cozy—but to show your deeply generous, your magnanimous nature and your lofty fellow-feeling you'll grovel on the floor."

"Myra, please," said Solomon, without effect.

"Look around you at the way we live," she cried, "this pigpen which can't be kept up together for five minutes no matter how I work—that's what your honesty has done for us, not only in this place but in three colleges before this. Look—" holding up three fingers as if the number had a special significance—"three colleges, where you went around like the righteous man himself, like Socrates from the Grand Concourse, insulting everybody right and left and using the Old Testament for a chest protector, you professional Jew, you."

She took a deep breath. Charles fidgeted very uneasily. Solomon, though pale, made no attempt to say anything. Perhaps, Charles thought, he is used to this; but it sounds as if her particular kettle has been on the edge of boiling for so long that there is nothing for it to do but begin to whistle and screech in this way.

"And I stood for all that," she resumed more quietly, in a dark yet piercing voice. "I stood for it and better than that I backed it up, not only because it was my

169

husband but because I admired you for it, too, like an idiot— Look at my Leon, I said, like any Mommy, Look at my Leon, he's been kicked out of another college. What intellect, what brilliance, how he sees through everybody. How honest he is.

"And now it's too late, now that you've cleverly arranged everything so that you could never have a career if you grew horns like Moses—now he says I take it all back, forget it, it's not important, let's all be friends. When we got married you had some sort of future, you perpetual brilliant young man, you. Now you've got nothing left but that marvelous honesty, which I've watered with my sweat year after year—and now, as God is my judge, you'll keep it."

Turning to Charles, she said, "On that basis we don't need your friendship, Mr. Osman. You should not have offered it on those terms. He is not going to change his decision—which has already cost me a day of moaning and groaning and aspirin and sympathy—and I don't care what he promised you, I promised nothing. If there is one word more said about it, I'll report your football player to the proper authorities myself."

"I hope you won't do that," said Charles.

"I know what you hope," she said bitterly.

Leon said to Charles, "I'm sorry you had to see this."

And she said, also to Charles, "You see his loyalty, don't you?"

The doorbell rang.

"Myra, go see who it is," said Leon.

"I won't," she said. "If it was the angel of the Lord himself, he could stay outside so far as I'm concerned."
170

"I'll go then." Solomon pulled his bathrobe up together, tightened the cord with a decisive gesture and went down the hall. Charles and Myra looked at one another and said nothing. As the door opened, after another long ring at the bell, and Solomon fell back before the new visitors, Charles saw that, as he had anticipated nervously for some minutes, Herman Sayre and Senator Stamp had become impatient of waiting any longer for his call and had taken things into their own hands. Behind them, like the charioteer Socrates spoke of, who had awkwardly in hand the two yoked horses of the soul, came President Nagel, an expression of nervous anguish on his face, as though he were (as well he might be, thought Charles) sick to the stomach.

Charles smiled angrily at Myra Solomon.

"Lift up your heads, O ye gates," he said, "and be lifted up, ye everlasting doors, for the king of glory enters in."

"Who is the king of glory?" she responded in scornful antiphony.

"He is on the side of the big battalions," said Charles.

2

The process of reasoning and rising temper which had brought the Senator and Mr. Sayre to Mr. Solomon's house, and made the President their unwilling follower, might be conjectural, but there was no need to conjecture on its strong foundation of bourbon whisky; it was clear at once to Charles that the two leaders at least were on the verge of being drunk (probably President Nagel, as their host, had been forced to keep up), and it merely remained to discover whether they were mean drunks or happy ones, with the immediate evidence heavily favoring the former chance.

To begin with, Leon Solomon did not greet the newcomers with any particular hospitality, and might even have slammed the door in their faces had they not more or less slammed it back and him with it in their advance.

"We're coming in," said Mr. Sayre much as a sheriff would do in a Western movie, and Senator Stamp added, "It will be better for you, young man, if you don't stand in the way." Their momentum took them down the hall to confront for an instant Charles and Mrs. Solomon; after an exchange of scowls they turned off into the living room, where presently everyone else had to follow. President Nagel, stopping with Solomon by the door, had succeeded in producing only an apologetic expression of the mouth and shoulders.

"This is my house," Leon was at last able to say, in a rising voice. "You have no right to come in here." She's right, thought Charles, he probably does have hysterical fits.

"This house is college property," said Mr. Sayre.

"And I'll thank you to keep your feet off my children's toys," cried Leon with great ferocity. "I swear to God you will pay for every ten-cent plastic Cadillac. I mean it," he added unnecessarily.

This threat made apparent something rather odd about the scene itself; there was no place to sit. Since

172

nobody would risk the loss of dignity entailed by sinking into one of the webbed chairs, and since—as in the problem of the goat, the wolf and the cabbages—no three persons were sufficiently compatible to share the couch, everyone had to stand up, and because of the litter on the floor one could not pace up and down and in fact had to be extremely cautious about even taking a step. So they all stood immobile as wax figures in some historic scene and glared at one another.

Suddenly Mrs. Solomon dropped to her knees and furiously began to scrabble toys and shoes up together.

"Myra, don't you touch those things!" shouted Leon, and she stopped but stayed just where she was, on her knees.

"What a place," muttered Mr. Sayre, looking around him.

"Do you want me to be ashamed?" Myra cried out. "Look at this room."

"No, I don't want you to be ashamed," her husband cried right back, in that same shrill voice. "They know why we live this way. We live this way because we are hired help. They are the ones who should be ashamed."

"Oh, come now," President Nagel said helplessly, and everyone looked at him but he did not offer to add to this exhortation.

"My dear lady," said Senator Stamp, bowing (or perhaps only bulging slightly) with excessive dignity. "My dear lady, allow me." He belched, and sat down on the floor, where he too began to gather together, very slowly, cars and planes and socks. Poor man! The urbanity and courtesy of the gesture was matched exactly by

173

his incompetence to make it. Being drunker than he had thought, perhaps, he almost at once gave up the collection of things and simply sat there unable to rise or, indeed, do much more than look stupidly about him.

Leon Solomon at this moment laughed, a high, neighing sound which seemed to Charles clearly the next thing to hysteria.

"You are laughing at a Senator of the United States," Mr. Sayre said. "Here, Josie, try to get up, there's a good man. Come, Harmon, give a hand—and if you look at me once more that way, as if you didn't want to admit you knew me," he suddenly shouted, "I'll break your goddamn contract."

Together, with a great deal of strain, the two of them got Senator Stamp on his feet and over to the couch, where he subsided more or less in a heap.

"I count four toys broken," said Leon in a threatening way. "Myra, get up off the floor." And then he added, "Four miserable rotten toys," and looked as if he might cry.

Myra got up and put her face very close to Leon's.

"Don't you dare cry," she said between her teeth, "don't you dare shed a single tear."

Leon said nothing but walked determinedly from the room and came back half a minute later with a glass two-thirds full of straight whisky in his hands; from this he proceeded to sip, delicately but almost continuously.

"Now this has got to stop," said Charles in a loud voice meant to be menacing and full of authority.

"Who says so?" Mr. Sayre demanded, raising his head from an inspection of the Senator.

"I say so," said Charles, and they glared at each other like small boys.

"You say so," Mr. Sayre said after a moment of this, "You—say—so. Mister, don't think I've forgotten you."

"How memorable can one get," said Charles with a sneer.

"You'll find out. When I've finished with you you'll wish you could get forgotten. I'll blackball you in every college in the country."

"Beginning with this one?"

"Yes, beginning with this one."

"I can see you doing it, too."

"People don't talk to me the way you talked to me, and especially people like you, *Professor*."

"How pleased you're going to be, then," Charles said, "to have me for a son-in-law." He smiled sweetly.

"What's that?" Mr. Sayre seemed even physically to go off balance, back on his heels. "Don't make me laugh," was at last the feeble reply he found.

"I don't care if you weep," said Charles.

"Gentlemen, really," President Nagel broke in, "we'll all be sorry for this if we go on. Remember what we came for, please."

"Never mind what we came for," Mr. Sayre said, and then, to Charles, with drunken concentration, "If you've laid a finger on my girl—" He got very red in the face and stopped, then with elaborate carelessness said to President Nagel, "I didn't know you encouraged the hired help to fool with the customers, Doctor."

Charles said, "I'll discuss this matter with anyone whose business it is, at another time and in another

175

place. Right now, I merely suggest to you, all three of you, that the best thing you could do is apologize to Mr. and Mrs. Solomon, and withdraw."

"Apologize?" moaned the Senator, holding his head in both hands.

"Apologize," roared Mr. Sayre, "apologize—to this subversive here, this creep, this—this Elder of Zion!"

"I guess there's no point in your apologizing now," said Charles evenly, "since you've just been unforgivable. I'm Jewish too, by the way," he added. "Contemplate that when you are feeling better. It'll make you feel worse."

He turned to address President Nagel.

"Since you seem relatively the sane member of your party," he said, "I will tell you that your visit was not necessary. Mr. Solomon consented, as a personal favor to me, to let your prize package play in the game tomorrow."

"He did not!" Mrs. Solomon cried just as Leon lifted his mouth from the glass and said, "That's all off, Osman."

"I don't blame you," said Charles, "I don't blame you a bit."

"I see now the way it was," Leon said. "They sent you over first, to try to get around me in a friendly way. Then if you didn't make it they brought up the heavy guns. They just got worried you hadn't made it—that's all. A little error, wouldn't you say? Since in five minutes you'd have been out of here and on the phone to let the bosses know what an easy mark I was."

"Oh sure," said Charles, "you can see what great buddies we are, all of us. Sure."

176

"Do you deny it?"

Charles was unable to deny it.

Mrs. Solomon now suddenly spoke up.

"Now I'm going to say something," she said decisively.

"You mustn't," cried Charles.

"I promised, dear," said Leon, "and we must always keep our promises, or we won't go to heaven when we're put through the gas chamber."

"Your football game," Mrs. Solomon continued, "your darling, lovely football game—is a crooked fake. That's all I wanted to tell you gentlemen—that, and how funny I think it all is."

The Senator suddenly lifted his head.

"Young woman," he said, "that is a very serious allegation. You should not make statements of that nature."

A child's voice came from the stairway in the hall: "Mommy and Daddy, Mommy and Daddy," in a rising, urgent singsong.

"Now you've got the children up," said Leon with final bitterness.

"What is it, Debbie?" called Mrs. Solomon, going into the hall.

"We can't sleep, we all got up again. There are people outside shining lights in, and sort of singing."

Turning and drawing aside the living-room curtain, Charles saw that the child's observation was perfectly accurate. There were people outside, quite a lot of them, some with torches; a car had been drawn up across the road so that the headlights shone over the porch and through the window and front door; and those people were sort of singing, a low, half-disorganized yet rhythmical muttering chant of which the words were not distinguishable.

Because the headlights of that car were shining in his eyes Charles found it hard to make out details. The flaring torches would now and then briefly stoop to illuminate a few faces—young, meaningless faces not particularly menacing, boys and girls one or two of whom he thought he could recognize. The crowd did not seem especially large, either, though supported by a few uniformed members of the band, two of them carrying the bass drum which could be heard thumping with a kind of stolid determination. The two boys on stilts, no longer carrying the banner, were stalking aimlessly up and down the road, and in the distance the sky shone dull red over the bonfire still. Charles let the curtain fall back and turned to the room again.

"And now, Machiavelli," he said to Dr. Nagel, "what do you recommend?"

The President in his turn went to the window and looked out. Clearing his throat several times, he said, "I'm sure they don't mean any harm. It's just sport."

"They might be here to sing Christmas carols," Charles said, "but it's not Christmas."

Mrs. Solomon came back into the room carrying the youngest child. The older girl and boy, looking about them with sleep-bewildered eyes, clung about her skirts. As the group paused before President Nagel it looked like a poster for American Motherhood Week.

"Do something," Mrs. Solomon said fiercely to the President. "Do something."

"Leon," said Charles, "go phone the police—go ahead. Now."

Leon Solomon did not move, however, and indeed scarcely seemed to take in the sense of what was happening. It was plain to Charles that terrible and absurd fantasies were passing through the man's mind, and that if he should speak it would be about the Gestapo and the gas chamber rather than about the present situation, whose perils formed a sinister and serious parody of those historical nightmares, and had without doubt a remote, incredible possibility of leading to the same result. There is nothing more paralyzing, he reflected, than a paranoid attitude to dangers which really exist.

"If you won't, then I must," he said. "Where's the phone?"

At Leon's mute nod, he started for the hall. Herman Sayre stood in his way.

"Don't get all steamed up, all of you," he said. "You're exaggerating. It's only a pack of kids. Harmon, go out there and tell 'em to go home."

Some portion of the crowd now began a rhythmic clapping, and chanted monotonously, "Let Blent play," over and over. Senator Stamp, on the couch, raised his head dully.

"What's happening?" he asked.

President Nagel visibly pulled himself together, but still hesitated.

"What shall I say?" he asked. "About—you know, tomorrow?"

Mr. Sayre looked him up and down with some disgust.

"What are you scared of, a revolution?" he asked. "I'll handle it." With a decisive air he turned and headed down the hall. Those in the living room heard him open the door. The noise from outside increased, the chanting broke off, many people began to boo, and all this hullabaloo did not leave off until Mr. Sayre came in and shut the door.

"They threw their hot dogs at me," he said, wiping his face with a handkerchief. "They must have thought I was you," he added to Solomon.

"I'll call the cops," Charles said. This time it was Dr. Nagel who stopped him.

"Please," he said. "I realize this is my responsibility, and I must face it. Let's not get the police in this unless it's absolutely necessary."

"They will be useful," said Charles, "for counting the bodies. All right. But whatever you do, do it now."

President Nagel went out on the porch. The booing and so forth began again but died away presently as some of the students recognized authority.

"Will you stop crying *this minute?*" said Leon savagely to the little boy, and then remorsefully began patting his head and saying "there, there." Except for this and the child's continued sobs it was now silent in the room and outside. They could hear perfectly well what Dr. Nagel had to say.

"This disgraceful demonstration will cease at once," he began. "You are behaving like savages. This is a civilized community, and I won't have it. Try to remember that you are young ladies and gentlemen, not male and female gorillas. You ought to be ashamed. When you stop to think that you raised this—this—practically a riot, for nothing less trivial than a football game, you certainly will be ashamed."

"What about Blent?" someone asked from the crowd.

"Young man, I can't see you—turn those headlights off, now," said Dr. Nagel. "Young man, I don't know who you are, but I know you are not the President of this College, because I am."

There was some feeble laughter at this, and Nagel thereafter proceeded with a calmer assurance. Charles thought he sounded like a radio comedian who has the audience on his side at last.

"I want you to bear in mind, young man—and all you young ladies and gentlemen—that you do not make the policies of this institution. I do that, and I am not required to explain my decisions to you or to secure your approval for any course of action which seems to me appropriate. Do any of you wish to argue the point?"

A moment of muttering stillness followed. No one spoke out.

"I see we are in agreement, then, on that fundamental point. Do not forget it. Since your perhaps natural anxiety about a fellow student has led you to this disgraceful exhibition, I want to emphasize to you that it is not in deference to your wishes—not in the least—but in accord with academic policy that the matter you came about has been reviewed and cleared up."

Possibly the students did not take in the entire sense of so fancy a set of expressions, for they made no re-

181

sponse, and President Nagel added very severely, "You will no doubt be pleased to know that Raymond Blent is eligible to play in the Homecoming Game tomorrow."

A scattered sort of cheering went up at this, together with a few odd, inexplicable boos and jeers, perhaps from those who would rather have had a great commotion ending in failure than this quiet success.

What a grandstand player! thought Charles, feeling suddenly very tired.

"You will confine your gratification," said the President when the cheering died away, "within the bounds of civilization and decency. And you will remember, please, that the decision to let Blent play does not reflect upon any member of the faculty. Now, ladies and gentlemen, I bid you good evening and advise you not to linger in this neighborhood, since any student found on these premises after the next five minutes will have his or her name taken and be expelled from the College. I hope that is clear?"

There was a noise somewhere between grumbling and cheering, the bass drum began to beat loudly, someone blew a squawk on a trumpet, and President Nagel came back into the house, nervous and chilled but evidently pleased with himself.

"That's that," said Mr. Sayre briskly. "I'll hand it to you, Harmon, when you finally got going you went right on through. We could have stood here arguing all night."

"At least," the President said, "we've managed without the police, and without the newspapers. They're children, really," he added, with an affectionate glance toward the window, "not an ounce of harm, only high spirits a bit out of hand."

There was a small sound of breaking glass; something hit the living-room curtains and fell to the floor. Charles went over to pick it up. It was a rock.

"Not an ounce of harm in it," he said, weighing this missile on his hand.

Leon Solomon stood in the center of the room and stared at the President.

"I resign from the College," he said.

"I'm sorry you feel that way," Dr. Nagel said, frowning. "If you really feel you must— But sleep on it, Solomon. Don't do anything now. We're all tired."

"Let him go," said Mr. Sayre easily, "it's the best way, let him go."

Charles said, "You can have my resignation too. I don't have any choice."

"Don't be such a hero," said Mr. Sayre. "Simmer down."

"Charles," said Dr. Nagel, "I hope you don't mean that. What I've done no doubt seems arbitrary and maybe opportunist as well, but at least this situation is finished. Perhaps in a calmer mood you will reconsider? I do hope so."

"It is not finished," cried Mrs. Solomon. "Remember what I'm telling you, your football game is crooked and your star player has been bought."

"Mrs. Solomon," the President said gravely, "I realize you're overwrought, we all are. We're none of us in a fit state to discuss any such charge at this time. Besides, I think that in a calmer mood, tomorrow maybe, when you've thought it over, you will decide that you are mistaken. You may even wish to withdraw the accusation; I would think it the generous thing to do."

"I don't want to be a bother," said Charles, "but does any of you smell something burning? Paint, maybe?"

Everyone began sniffing the air earnestly. Charles seized up the blanket from the couch, awakening and half-upsetting the Senator, and rushed down the hall to the door.

One of those torches lay flaming on the wooden floor outside. It took only a moment or so for Charles to cover the oil-soaked rags with the blanket and stamp vigorously up and down till the fire was out. It left a black burned patch on the porch floor, that was all. There were no students to be seen anywhere.

The others had crowded helpfully to the front door, where they stood watching, and to them Charles said, "Full of high spirits, ain't they? The local papers will be delighted. Students Riot, Stone Teacher. Torch Scorches Porch."

"The papers need not know about it," said Dr. Nagel.

"Oh, I might tell them myself," Charles said carelessly, and straightened up to look first at the President, then at Herman Sayre. "I don't know, though," he said wearily, "it's hardly worth it. I'm bored with the lot of you. You're crooks, but you're such cheap crooks. You'll always win, I guess, but what you win always looks like a dog-turd on the rug after you win it. I can see in your faces that you're pleased. A little anxious maybe, because you've been caught with your fingers in the candy again, but pleased even so because you are winners. The captain of the *Ship of Fools*," he added, "and his first mate. Sail on, sail on."

"We should go now, I think," Dr. Nagel said to Mr. Sayre. To Solomon he said, "Mr. Solomon, I am deeply sorry for the behavior of our students. I apologize. Of course it goes without saying that the College will put any damage right, the blanket, the paintwork, the window. I'll have it seen to on Monday morning. And before you write out any resignation, come and have a talk with me. That goes for you too, Charles. Think it over."

Mr. Sayre said, "We'll have to help Josie to the car." To Charles and Leon he turned then and said, amazingly enough, "You've got spirit, both you men. I like that in a man, spirit. Don't worry about some of those things I said a while back. I get like that when I'm tight, everybody knows that, and they'll tell you old Sayre is not such a bad egg after all. Don't think you've got to resign on my account," he added, and then addressed himself to Charles alone. "As for what you've got going with my girl Lily, Dr. Osman, I'd just warn you—don't take Lily so seriously. She's a pretty wild sort of kid. She thinks she wants to marry lots of people."

He put out his hand. Charles refused to take it. Leon too turned away.

"Okay, okay," Mr. Sayre said. "You intellectuals are a proud lot. It don't mean much of anything, though."

Shortly after this, he and the President supported Senator Stamp down the stairs and into the night, while the others watched in unbroken silence.

"Well, dear God, that's that," Charles said when the car had driven away. "You see, they didn't believe you,"

185

he said to Myra Solomon, who merely looked at him angrily for an instant and then said, "I'll put the kids back in bed now."

Charles and Leon, left alone, went back to the kitchen and got drinks.

"The captains and the kings depart," said Charles. "Where to next, I wonder?"

"Are you really quitting?" Leon asked.

"Looks that way."

"You shouldn't do that on my account. Although," he added, "I guess you can get another job easily enough."

"It wasn't on your account," Charles said. "Just another bloody matter of principle."

"Are you really going to marry the girl?"

"I don't have any idea. I think to try."

"David and Bathsheba." A horn sounded outside.

"That'll be Lily now, probably," said Charles. "I must go. What do you mean, about David and Bathsheba?"

"I mean what Nathan the prophet said, Thou art the man. Setting Uriah in the forefront of the battle, and so on."

Charles looked at him curiously.

"It's not really much like that, is it?"

"I guess not." Leon laughed nervously. The horn blew again, and Charles finished his drink.

"Thank you for a most entertaining evening, Dr. Solomon," he said. "I can get my coat all right."

Leon said, "It won't make much difference whether we're friends or not, since we won't be here. I've forgiven you, Osman, but, you know, I think I resent you. I think I envy you. What kind of friendship could come from that?"

"It doesn't take an act of Parliament, you know," said Charles, "and I don't see what there is in me for you to envy."

"You know the world," said Leon. "You'll always be successful."

"Oh, I can see that from the show I put on tonight— and all day. *Nihil humanum a me alienum puto.* A great success, but he kept his gentle heart and deep goodness, and when he got angry his victims trembled as though they had been bitten by a hamster. Well, never mind, Leon, never mind. The nice thing about success these days is that it looks much the same as failure."

They shook hands in some sort of sentimental valediction, and Charles left just as the horn sounded impatiently for the third time.

3

The drive into town seemed to take longer than it had before, and perhaps it did, on account of patches of fog which had formed in the hollows of the highway. Lily, also, appeared to Charles to be very drunk, to the point at which she drove the car more slowly than before and quite awkwardly, with an excess of conscious precision, as though to demonstrate perfect control. Charles himself, though not drunk, had reached some other sort of reaction to excess, and scarcely cared what happened any more. Violent death on the highway, it seemed to him, might be the appropriate end to a day such as he had passed. Nevertheless it seemed proper to him to ask the girl if she did not think he ought to take charge. She did not.

"This car doesn't let anybody drive it but me," she said.

"You do drink quite a lot, don't you?" said Charles.

"Why, yes, I do," she said, as though he had revealed an interesting new notion, in which, however, she did not happen to be interested.

"Why do you?"

"Please don't be dull," she said, expressing her petulance not only by this remark but by a burst of speed which made Charles shut his eyes tight and wait for the end. She soon slowed down, though, as if bored with such gestures, and they drove along without further talk. Charles sank as deeply as possible, which was not any great depth, into the car, pulled his collar up around his ears, and demonstrated a courageous carelessness by pretending to fall asleep. Perhaps he did fall asleep for a few seconds now and then, for such thoughts as came into his mind would take sometimes their proper form as thoughts, then would slide abruptly into, say, newspaper headlines, shop windows, and, at last, into images from nowhere and everywhere, a series of them coherent at first but at length lapsing into disconnected pieces of violence one of which would shake him awake; whereon the process began again. This happened several times, and strengthened his impression that the drive of at most fifteen minutes continued interminably.

Charles found it in the first place quite pleasant, as it had never been that he could remember before, to be driven by someone else, and particularly by a drunken young goddess of innocent audacity (if that were correct) with whom he was in love. He gave himself up willingly to this feeling, to these feelings of helplessness, irresponsibility, and adoration. If now and then he looked over at that girl she seemed to him both glorious and pathetic, image of something most fragile, most expensive, breakable perhaps but scarcely attainable. Those fine eyes, so beautiful in concentration, were probably a trifle unfocused from drink; it would be years before all that began to show, wouldn't it? Or it might make no difference whatever, in the next instant. Lovers Meet Death in Highway Smash. The burning truck lay on its side, the sports car sort of squashed against its belly, pieces of Charles, pieces of Lily, lovers. Tragedy on West Road. Not what you are, but what people can be persuaded to think you were, Romeo and Juliet, Vronsky and Anna, David and Bathsheba, the Gumps, Pasiphae and the Bull. To have, to the limits of civil violence, that delicate body near him, that bewildering and perilous immediacy to grow in a dozen years dear, familiar, and dull (with hot water bottles and aspirin), or to be blown instantly out of the range of quarrels, moralities, principles and decisions—which was the reality?

A truck roared by backwards, red lights shining; they sped down a hill into fog and Lily braked hard. Charles sat up, then slumped back again as they resumed a steady pace.

Honest man, man of sense, man of principle and integrity, *honnête homme;* meanwhile one had resigned one's position, though not in an attitude of resignation. Had he really? And was it possible to say why? Blessed are the self-righteous, for they never doubt. History a Disappointment, Says Eminent Divine. Historian Finds World Not Good Enough. Resignation, resignation, recommended to the nobility and gentry by the better sort of philosopher, whose boils, cataracts, poverty, consumption, paresis merely demonstrate to the full his ability to afford the world. And age, sage age, what now of that? The slightly thinning hair, the Ovaltine at night beside the volume on the bedside table, the little loose and hanging pouches of the flesh hinting that gravity begins to win the long downward pull to the tomb. Ichabod, Ichabod, we are going, goddess, going. Brush your teeth twice a day, live a dying life, if the room is smoky leave it. Lesbia's sparrow got through, so can you. Throw away that truss, *il faut tenter de vivre.* In the stone stadium, the warriors, gladiators, Christian soldiers, do what they must do; go thou and do likewise, Charles aged twelve, having lost your football helmet (he gave it away to a nephew, actually), run staring into the timeless glass and straight-arm fiercely (which it is not now the fashion to do) the clenched face of the professor of history whom if you look closely you will discover there. What a roar goes up from the thousand thousand throats of angels and archangels, saints, martyrs, virgins, the alumni of this world who made it and look for you to do the same. Welcome to Avalon, Valhalla, and all the locker rooms thereof; take off your sweaty uniform, have a shower, and tell us how it all was: we were on dawn patrol, I had pneumonia, somebody must have pushed me. Lovers Meet Death in Highway Smash. Ambulances, police cars, lights, loud voices, then the smooth ride downstream in the glass-walled Cadillac, like the lily maid.

They stopped for a traffic light. The town was not much for night life and now, just a few minutes short of midnight, scarcely anything could be seen moving down the long main street except the series of traffic lights which passed through their solemn, orderly routine of changes and repetitions. Shop windows nevertheless blazed with lights, naked mannequins extended hands in delicate gestures of regret, like Eurydice bidding farewell, the complete bedroom sets, toy automobiles and wooden horses, the carpets tilted in display, the pyramid of thermos bottles, the male mannequin in green tweeds looking eagerly out at the street, all passed by silent and strange as tableaux in a dream.

Of course, Charles told himself, all this that happened today comes from trying to be good, trying to help others, trying to do the right thing; in a way, when one did that, one became unreliable; much as a driver would do who sought to anticipate the next move of another driver instead of simply assuming the worst. It was no paradox but the plain sense of things that the world could go insane from an excess of altruism and high-principled behavior as much as from greed and unprincipled selfishness (if selfishness were not, for that matter, a principle in itself). A man went after what he wanted, that was something; you could count on it. It

191

was when everyone began being—or even when some-one began being—*objective* that confusion set in. A deplorable idea? But there it was. It seemed as though there no longer existed in his mind any other idea but this one; not one idea worthy of—let us not say belief, reverence, honor—not one idea worthy of a short, nasty laugh, an apologetic cough, an unassuming shrug of the shoulders.

Men want riches—surely to God men want riches? Could one hold to that even if it seemed at times that men just as surely want the failure which lies in wait behind every success? Because here perhaps, after all, was the heroism that truly existed in this vale of tears; that men unflinchingly went on facing up to the noble pretense that what they wanted was success, when in truth they wanted nothing of the sort, when every success revealed itself—at once, before the testimonial dinner was over, or the ink had dried on the parchment of the diploma—as merely another piece of nonsense gained at the awful cost of having to defend it and things like it forever and ever; and not merely defend but somehow, at the same time, succeed and supersede; so that one was forever saying, and supporting the say-ing with one's breath, one's life, that this that one had was valuable, measurably if not immeasurably valuable, exactly in the degree that one at once held on to it and went beyond it. In all the attics were to be found the splintered hockey stick, the old radio, the schoolbooks, the pictures of the first girl friend; where the wife and the new Buick and the television and the children would as certainly follow.

What happened to people, then, if they fell through these fictions which held the civil world, or became the victims of those impermissible passions which everywhere await us, inside the refrigerator, behind the TV screen, at the suburban corner where the grand boulevard dies away into the wilderness?

Probably something like Lily happened, and happened, too, rather late in the day for heroic extravagance, after one had spent a considerable number of years living, believing, defending and even—Lord help us—teaching the correct fictions with all the energy, courage, endurance and (bless us) honesty one had. What a shame that just after one had at so considerable expense *formed one's character,* as educators say, and was ready to drink Ovaltine every night till time ended, life should again appear, approach with a smile of surprise (as though she had not been waiting in the wings) that the orderly world should begin slowly to collapse, and say, "Are you a man of sense?"

Afterward, probably, one went away, far away, to another town, changed one's name, took some simple job in hand, and lived quietly to the end, known to one's neighbors only for a queer, meaningless smile.

Aged Recluse Dies. Mr. Crawfurd Osp—they never change the initials on the pigskin bag—long known to local citizens simply as Perfesser, died last night in Mercy Hospital. His age was unknown. Neighborhood children were bored to tears by the tiny wooden footballs he used to whittle and give them on their birthdays. The whereabouts of living relatives, if any, are unknown. Around Mr. Osp's neck when he died was a silver locket which when opened proved to contain a canceled three-cent stamp. The significance of all this is most unclear; if history consists of the inside of the outside, the revelation of some enduring realities on the human scene, then this is not history and will be buried in an unmarked grave in the Potter's Field, if we have such a thing.

Or if not that, the other course was clear: to stop being one's brother's keeper, or the keeper at any rate of his conscience, and be for oneself. Not merely to accept life, an idea having in it a kind of academic condescension, but to seize it by its golden chain, muss its hair, tear off the funereally lascivious gown, embrace, kiss (as though seeking to eat) the white skin which thinly held in some furious, insane spirit (in civil affairs named Lily, otherwise anonymous though unique) without which it was impossible to live: wreck, ruin, make, mate, in the one original incorporation where personal property reached its end, turned both backs upon the world and in one constructive rape irresponsibly assumed the guilt of the future. Which was as much as to say, what was on the point of being said for so long, would the great game be lost and that boy really destroy himself? An absurd idea, but the absurd did not lie far off. The wish, the dream, the will, were all; sin lieth at the door. Or if the game were won, would the hero be destroyed by professional criminals from the Big City? The wish is father to the man, the family man with the wounded brow, out there in the Land of Nod where legends end.

At the foot of the main street they turned down past the railroad station, where life continued even at this hour, blazing with lights and the smoke of two or three engines whose great iron clangor under the sheds filled Charles with unidentifiable memories, fusions of memory, the nostalgia and boredom of waiting rooms. A couple of blocks further the neon sign of Nick's Railroad Grill flashed on and off. It was a large wooden house, standing alone on its side of the street—there were high, blank walls of warehouses across the way— in a desolation of vacant lots and what seemed to be tall hills of coal. Its isolation in the scene gave it for Charles the quality of a stage set, a piece of some Potemkin Village behind which, clearly, there could be nothing real, nothing but struts and lashings, stage-hands lounging and actors and actresses nervously waiting for cues which perhaps no one would ever give. A sinister stage set, though.

"You should never have come down here," he said as Lily stopped the car. "I can't leave you outside, though I don't much want to take you in. But don't stare at people, and don't make remarks. They may be criminals in there, but we're not supposed to make any particular point of it. And, darling—do try to look a little less beautiful."

"Charles," she said, "are you frightened for my virtue?"

"That's another thing, too," he said. "I don't know if we can bring this off, even now. They may simply tell me to go to hell. But whether it works or doesn't, this is my last attempt to help your boy. After that, he's on his own. And so am I," he added, looking her boldly in the eye.

"You scare me, dear," Lily said, shuddering elaborately. "And you needn't keep calling him *my* boy. You're so serious, Professor, and so full of good intentions."

"That title of Professor, silly as it is, has become even more of a formality since I saw you last. But I'll tell you about that later. Let's get this thing over with."

The inside of the Railroad Grill was comfortably hot, stuffy and even domestic, since the heat came principally from an old-fashioned pot-bellied stove at the far end of the room; but Charles had come instinctively prepared to find every circumstance criminal, and the most innocent items of furniture, not to mention the human beings, caused him to frown: the two old men in the corner playing checkers and wearing striped railroading caps, for example. Checkers, indeed! Railroading caps, forsooth! When one had inside knowledge, these disguises were quickly penetrated. The three boys in black leather jackets lounging by the bar were clearly juvenile delinquents, if not actually gunmen. Two old ladies drinking beer at a table covered with newspapers: whores, off-duty. Or if too old for that (on second look), they must be madams. Unsuccessful ones. And so on.

Naturally everyone in the place looked up at the new arrivals, and there were several whistles, perhaps as much at Charles as at Lily.

They went to the bar, which was also a very domestic sort of thing, being half bar and half lunch counter, with coffee urns, glass-covered plates of old doughnuts, menus stood up between salt and pepper. The barman, from whom as a matter of form they ordered drinks, looked rather like a schoolteacher, Charles thought, with tired, delicate features and a pince-nez which was loose and had constantly to be pushed back on the bridge of his nose, a gesture he made so often and unconsciously that he had to do everything else with one hand. He was not even wearing a white jacket or an apron, but a plain business suit.

"We've come to see Max," said Charles, after they had been served. He was pleased with himself for the casual way in which he got off this conspiratorial phrase, as in a foreign language, and felt at any rate that it gave him some status in the sight of those three *youths* (falling back on Rover Boy parlance) standing beside him.

"He's in the back, through the kitchen," the barman said, pointing. "He'll see you—alone, though," he said as Charles began to steer Lily in that direction.

"Oh," said Charles, dismayed, and stopped. He could not offend these possibly dangerous people by indicating in any way that they were unfit company for a young lady; surely, at all events, nothing could happen. He looked at Lily.

"Stay right here," he said, and whispered in addition, "Don't look at people and don't drink any more than that one."

She smiled at him in a kind of loose-mouthed way which he found attractive but not especially trustworthy, and he left.

What Charles found when he had passed through the steaming kitchen, with its black iron stove and one cook who mutely indicated a door, was a room with one curtained window and a table and two chairs, in one of which a man sat smoking a thin cigar. Indeed, the only other furnishing of this room was an ash tray in front of the man. He wore a polo coat, but otherwise did not very exactly correspond to the description given by Raymond Blent. Hard to tell, though, about the hair, as this man kept his gray fedora on his head, and sat hunched over the table, his coat dragging on the floor, as though he had only recently arrived and did not expect to be here long.

"Mr. Max?" said Charles with unnecessary politeness.

"Max," the other said, barely taking the cigar from his mouth.

It was plain, at least, that he was not Jewish; that was something. Italian, rather. But of course he might not be, probably was not, the same man who had approached Blent. There seemed, even, something familiar about the face—Charles had seen it before, and he enjoyed a momentary wild fantasy of identifying this man, which would lead to the arrest of the other members of the gang (for this one would squeal) and what one could call the cracking of the case wide open. Absent-minded Professor No Dope. Historian Uses Head. Except that Charles could not, not now anyhow, identify the man; perhaps there was some passing resemblance, indeed, to one of his colleagues.

"You know why I'm here," said Charles, drawing out the other chair and sitting down. He too kept his coat and hat on, and reflected that the movies had established every convention of this conventional sort of interview; perhaps there was a bodyguard in the closet.

"I don't know nothing," the other man said. "Let's keep it that way."

"But I naturally thought you were—you would be—" Charles broke off in some chagrin, not wishing to say outright anything like "one of the crooks," "a member of the syndicate" or anything of that sort. "How do I know I'm dealing with the right people?" he asked.

"You don't," said Max. "Nobody invited you, you invited yourself."

Charles briefly envisioned this remark as it would look on his tombstone: Nobody invited him, he invited himself.

"Now look," he said, "prudence is all very well, but it can be carried too far. If everyone behaved in this way, no business could be done at all."

The other man wearily shrugged his shoulders.

"I was just told to wait here for the money you would give me," he said.

"Ah, you do know that? We're getting somewhere, then." Charles got out his wallet and deliberately started to count out twenty-dollar bills, laying each one on the table as he did so.

"There," he said when he had finished. "You understand what that's for, don't you?"

The other man removed the cigar from his mouth and stared at Charles for a long moment. He shook his head sadly, and said, "Professor, you got a lot of faith in human nature."

"Aha, you know who I am, too."

"Let's never mind," Max said, "what I know and what I don't. I just meant, I never saw somebody come in cold and put five hundred fish on the table to a guy he never saw before, is all I meant."

Looked at in this way, Charles could see, his behavior might be called a trifle absurd. He put his hand on the stack of bills and in an access of meaningless efficiency demanded a receipt. The other grinned, nodded, took a crumpled piece of notepaper from his pocket, borrowed Charles's pen and wrote, simply and without meaning: "Rec'd sum of $500.00. Max."

"A lot of good that is," Charles said. "You should put what it's for."

"You don't know what it's for," Max said patiently. "Nobody promised it would buy you anything. It was your idea, remember. I was told to tell you," he added, "that you should not count too much on anything. Things are the way they are anyhow, maybe."

Charles said with indignation, "I know what I hope to accomplish. If you accept this money, then I take it you accept, or your employers or your friends accept, the meaning behind it: that things are what they were before, before this money changed hands—and all bets are off. It's as though this miserable thing—you know quite well what I mean—had never happened."

"You say, Professor," Max replied. "You're doing it, I ain't."

"All right, suppose I simply take the money back and walk out?"

"Go ahead. It's not my money. I just run errands around here."

"No," Charles said, mostly to himself, defeated.

"That's no good. I have to take the chance, don't I? Here—" He pushed the bills across the table decisively. "I've done the best I could, and what's more," he added, fixing Max with a stern glance, "my responsibility in all this is now at an end."

"Nice if you feel all comfortable," said Max. He swept up the money and stuffed it carelessly in his overcoat pocket, keeping his fist rammed down on it. Charles meanwhile folded the receipt and put it away in his wallet.

"Good night," Max said, not moving. He stared without expression until Charles, feeling helpless enough, went back the way he came, through the kitchen and into the barroom, where Lily, leaning elegantly if precariously on the bar, was in lively conversation with those three sinister youths in black leather jackets.

With a high disregard for all this, Charles said to the barman, "I'll pay for the drinks now."

The bill seemed somewhat large, and he stared at it, frowning.

"We bought a round for the boys," Lily said. "And of course I had one more."

"Do you have to go now, Lily?" one of these boys plaintively said.

Charles paid the bill without comment, took Lily by the arm and steered her, with a firmness only just short of violence, toward the door.

"Good night, Lily," cried the three young men after them, and one added, loud and clear, "Good night, Dr. Osman."

"You had to give them our names?" Charles said furiously, when they had got outside. "Haven't you any discretion at all?"

Lily shook her arm free, gave him an angry look, and then began to laugh.

"You don't want me to be a snob, do you?" she demanded. "The little pimply one took Eighteenth Century French Lit. the same year I did."

Charles realized glumly that he had absolutely failed to look at the faces of those three lads, whom quite possibly he had taught in class. Lily's amusement did not much improve his temper.

"Darling Charles, you are funny," she cried, staggered a bit, came to a stop. "You know," she said with an odd expression, "I think I am just a little drunk. It's against my principles, but you had better drive." She handed him the key and when they were in the car snuggled close to him, with her head on his shoulder.

"I think I got young Mr. Blent off the hook," Charles said. "At least, I don't know what all else I could have done. I gave back the money—what could be clearer than that?"

"I just don't know," muttered Lily.

"It's too late to tell him tonight," Charles said. "But I want you to tell him, call him up, tomorrow. I wash my hands of the whole business, understand. He ought to know he's in the clear, or as near as can be managed, but there's no reason for me to have to let him know."

Charles suffered from that slight rigidity of character which makes a man allow that if he does another a good turn he need not be especially gracious about it;

besides, he would be rather pleased to have Blent understand that he, Charles, had been with Lily, and that they had *discussed everything.*

"Will you do that?" he insisted. "Will you be responsible for that?"

"Tomorrow, darling," she murmured sleepily.

"Where do you live?" he asked. "I'll drive you home."

Lily gave her address—it was out a way, almost in the suburbs—and seemed to go to sleep while Charles undertook to get her there. He had had, alas, no experience at all with these low-slung new sports models, which are so agile they seem alive—this one jumped like a cat at his touch—and though he felt on the one hand pleased with himself, the responsible yet audacious gentleman, learned, courteous, capable at the wheel of his Bugatti with a lovely girl beside him (as in an advertisement for gracious living) he also felt a good deal of nervous tension at each corner. When they reached the region of Lily's home he shook her awake and she gave, rather drowsily, directions which brought them at last to a great mansion among trees, and he turned in at the driveway.

Unhappily this quite sharp turn came off not so well. The car, responding eagerly to his somewhat heavy pressure on accelerator and wheel, scraped loudly against a stone pillar at the entry and then, in consequence of his rapid overcorrection, climbed the high curb opposite with the offside front wheel. The underside shrieked as it scored the stone, and they came to a stop all tilted and askew.

"Oh, dear," was what Charles found to say.

Lily got out and stood on the walk looking thoughtfully at the car.

"I'm very sorry," Charles said.

"The poor dear must have resented you," she said, and laughed sadly. "Never mind, leave it and come in for a nightcap, darling. Someone will do something about it in the morning."

"Of course I am responsible for any damage," Charles formally announced.

"Oh, Charles, do forget it," she said with a flash of anger. "You fool," she added under her breath, so that he could not be certain (though he imagined) what the word had been.

When they had walked the few steps to the door and gone in, they stood in the front hall. The house was silent, with an effect of vast, dark spaces everywhere beyond the little lighted area around them. When she turned to him, dropping her cloak on the floor, he saw tears in her eyes. She put her arms around him and they embraced as if helplessly for as much as a minute.

"Charles, I'm so miserably unhappy," she moaned. "Help me, please."

These words filled him with a pity and tenderness, desire also, with which he saw, just then, nothing to do. Help her—sexually? Was that her meaning?

"I'll do anything I can, darling," he whispered gently, patting her naked shoulder.

They stood apart suddenly, by consent of both of them, and she swayed uncertainly back toward him. Charles felt her weight, rather greater than he would have supposed, go dead in his arms. It was a moment both wanton and gross; he was uncertain at first whether her fall represented desire or incompetence. Nor was this doubt cleared up when she sagged still more heavily against him, whispering at the same time, "Make love to me now, now, quickly."

Awkwardly Charles managed to get his arm under her behind and, with considerable effort, grunting, swing her aloft, where he stood, in the posture of a heroic rescuer from some sea disaster, not knowing which way to go in the darkness all around. Lily's head sagged back away from him, and he thoughtfully kissed her taut throat, as though this were something to do while waiting. She responded by whispering, sadly rather than lasciviously, some obscene words, and since his arms began to feel the strain terribly, Charles walked with her toward an open archway in the gloom.

Fortunately the first thing he bumped into was the back of a couch, so that as he suddenly bent forward and had to let the girl go she merely rolled gently onto the soft pillows, over once, and, still gently, to the floor. Charles found a lamp on an end table and lit it, then heaved the girl's body, one end at a time, back up on the couch, where he sat down next to her.

The top of that funereal gown, miraculously supported until now upon mere nubility and the power of the flesh, had come undone somewhere and peeled back, exposing her left breast, not to mention Raymond Blent's fraternity pin. Charles touched the breast; the nipple erected itself.

"Hurt me, please, please, please," Lily murmured, together with a few other things, and seemed to fall asleep.

"You're very drunk," Charles said accusingly. "It wouldn't be right—it wouldn't even be pleasure." He stood up and waited uncertainly, as though for a sober and rationally worded invitation. The girl's eyes remained closed, her head lolled back, her face seemed very pale, she said no word.

Charles waited a moment longer. Surely she had passed out, but why with that smile on her face? He went out to the hall, picked up her cloak and came back. Her breathing was heavier, was it? More regular than before? He stood there looking down on her, then with something like reverence laid the cloak over her nakedness. After a moment more he turned out the light and left the house.

No sooner was he out the door and down the walk—where that automobile's headlights, reflecting the light from the house, seemed to look at him critically and with some derision—than he began to feel absolutely enraged, at Lily and at himself.

What else, though, was he to have done? One did not rape, even by invitation, a drunken, unconscious female. Was she that drunk, though? Was she unconscious? He began to have doubts—even though, or especially because, she was all one wanted in the entire world. How dare she withdraw from the situation in that graceless fashion—how dare she leave him alone?

With this feeling, at the same time, there contended a good deal of sexual pride. She loves me, he told himself, there's the proof of it, she gave herself absolutely, shamelessly and absolutely.

Except that she didn't, as it had turned out. Had he been foolish? Was she testing him? By now, perhaps, she had sat up, sad, angry, amused—who could tell what her response might be?—and gone up to bed. He turned back to the house, but no lights had gone on upstairs.

Her old man might have come in, too, at that moment. At least, Charles was proud to reflect, he had not withdrawn on that account. Should he go back? He hesitated, then decided sadly that he would end by waking the whole house, remembered that at the age of twenty or so he would have had no hesitation, under like circumstances, in doing exactly that, or chancing it, and at last walked decisively away.

It took him some fifteen minutes' walking to reach an avenue and an all-night gas station where he phoned for a cab. Responsible to the last, he made the driver take him not directly home but to the street, still noisy with parties, where he had left his car so many hours before. Like any mature citizen after a night of cautious excess, Charles drove his car into its garage and went upstairs to his rooms, slowly, wearily, soberly, and with the beginning of a slight, retributive headache. It had been a long day.

5

Of thousands of people sitting around the stadium on this brilliant November afternoon, Charles Osman was certainly the only one who believed himself to have personally guaranteed, so far as any man could, the honesty of the game. This belief, of which he was, to be sure, only intermittently conscious, had raised to a new power the nervous intensity of his feelings about football generally, so that, just as in his undergraduate days, he was unable to eat his lunch or, indeed, pay attention to much of anything else. He had walked past the stadium a number of times, telling himself it was ridiculous to be so before-handed, and suddenly, three-quarters of an hour before game time, as early as the gates were opened, in fact, he had gone in, bought an inordinately expensive and glossy souvenir program—something he generally did not do—and taken his place in the mediocre seat to which as a faculty member he was entitled: about halfway up on the home team's side, between the twenty-five- and the thirty-yard lines.

His purpose in buying the program had been to assure himself that Raymond Blent was indeed in the starting line-up; and so he was, bearing the number seven, standing six feet and one inch, weighing one hundred and eighty-three pounds. Of course Charles realized at once that the sort of assurance the program gave, since it must have been printed a fortnight before, was purely formal, official, and so to say historical; yet such was his nervousness that he would not readily have done without this piece of paper. Also, by coming early, he was enabled to watch the practice sessions of both teams and there, since the players appeared without helmets, identify Raymond Blent for himself and make sure (as though suspecting up to the last minute some trick) that he was wearing the number seven as certified in the program. It remained to see that he would play, but of this Charles now felt reasonably certain, since there would otherwise be no point whatever in the boy's appearing at all.

The sky was a pure blue; the sun, already halfway down the sky, concentrated its royal golden light in the circle of the stadium and on the immaculate, measured green whose intervals were marked in white. The field itself had a kind of totemic or sacrificial appearance, a ground to be kept inviolate on all profane occasions, then to be torn up by one fury only; even the players seemed aware of this quality, when they came out walking delicately as Agag; they sniffed the cold, bright air, tested the spring of the ground with a toe, danced a few tentative, mincing steps before first digging their cleats into the new green space which belonged to them and finally throwing themselves down, rolling around, turning somersaults—actions which no doubt had a rational purpose of warming-up and reducing tension but which reflected also some new, delightedly innocent relation with the earth itself. Their uniforms, the red and white on one side, black and white on the other, made the same effect of brilliant purity, of cleanliness carefully preserved for the one ceremonial destruction.

For his part, Charles, accustomed to taking long views, felt already something of the melancholy which was the inevitable outcome of all this excitement; that this game, which seemed to stand brilliant and secure in the very path of time, an occasion, an event, a something of magnificent solidity devised by the wit of man to make the sun and moon stand still, was doomed to be itself merely a part of time; that for its two hours' impression of timeless vigor, immortal and anonymous youthfulness, time exacted its usual price; which only the historian, perhaps, was condemned to be gloomy about in advance.

He had not slept well the night before, and still suffered from a little, wandering headache, scarcely so much a physical pain as a feeling of mental remoteness, a tendency of the eyes to blur out of focus as though simply refusing their attention to mere spectacle and showing an undefined wish to see something else. Charles now and then was confusedly reminded of having dreamt very numerous and very fatiguing dreams during his broken sleep, and felt (though he could remember little or nothing of all that) as though he had come here from a long, futile, miserable life spent elsewhere.

Well before game time the stadium was nearly full. The players retired to their dressing rooms; the band, in red jackets and white trousers and caps, paraded up and down the field, going sturdily from tonic to dominant and back with a fine resonance of thumps and blares and booms and a fine reflection of the light from their golden horns; six drum majorettes, high-stepping with naked knees and black boots, went before, twirling, twisting, tossing and catching their batons. It seemed as though everyone began to roar, and yet as though no individual had any part in the sound produced. Charles made no noise, the people around him seemed not to be making any particular noise, yet the sound continued to roll out in waves; one felt that *something,* not necessarily human, had begun to roar. The band formed itself up before the visiting team's side and played *their* "Alma Mater"; then came back to the home side and played *their* "Alma Mater": two solemn, mournful airs which, harmonically at any rate, were hardly to be distinguished one from the other; yet when so addressed the graduates and undergraduates of each institution stood solemnly up, held felt hats

211

against their chests, and sorrowfully sang. Many an eye was wet.

What in the world could it all be for? Charles glanced impatiently at the clock on the scoreboard, which told him nothing since it was designed to measure the game alone, and therefore had not begun to move. What a heroic view of time! That clock would move, during the afternoon, only during the instants of (allowing for a nicety of legal definition) actual play; when either side felt that things were going wrong, or had gone far enough for the moment, the clock would be stopped: *time* would be *out*. That clock, in fact, since it measured at no time any space of time greater than fifteen minutes, did not need (and did not have) a hand to tell the hour; that hour of which one might paradoxically say, considering it from a certain point of view, that it was eternal while it lasted. It was hard to say, about football as about games in general, which was more impressive, the violence or the rationality; whether the more important element was the keen demonstration of hostility and aggressiveness (with consequent arguments, developed by Plato and Aristotle, as to whether such demonstrations intensified or harmlessly liberated those passions) or, quite the contrary, the demonstration of control, of order, plan, and human meaning in the universe. Orderly violence! Did that oxymoron define civilization? Surely, to begin with, order and violence had been, or been considered to be, opposites, and order was imposed as a means of doing away with violence, on the famed model, in the individual, of reason quelling the passions. But was there

212

in nature any violence so violent, so furious-cruel, as the violence of reason? Was any creature not gifted with reason capable of producing such orderly explosions of force as, say, the symphonies of Mozart or the advance of armies to the assault? The avowed ideals of society were measure and reason; measure and reason had made society in the image of an armed camp, until the model of its life, the city with its squared and numbered streets, betrayed itself as based however inefficiently (for history and tradition had moved blindly in this matter at many times) upon logistical considerations, to the end that an absolute force might be instantaneously (and in an orderly manner) mobilized.

It was this, then, that thousands of apparently good-natured citizens were here in the stadium to celebrate, the ideal maximum of violence, short of death or (it was hoped) serious injury, combined with the ideal maximum of the most pharisaical rationality and control. It would not do to say that people came to be entertained, for one had to ask at that point what it was that entertained people, and why of all things they were entertained by, particularly, this. Perhaps war itself, in its beginning, had been no more than such a ceremony as a football game, and scarcely more heroic or more dangerous than that village game of football anciently played in England, on Shrove-Tide Tuesday, where the unmarried women were always, by law, defeated by the married women. It might be—again the odd joke of history!—that the earliest form of war was predetermined as to its outcome, having a magical purpose and a ceremonial arrangement which, entering history as garbled traditions, were misinterpreted as both real and necessary: a nasty joke, if true. But civilization at present, and historically, depended on one decision and one decision alone: that it was better to sacrifice, at need, thousands and millions of men by accident—that is, in reality—than to sacrifice one man by pre-election—that is, ceremonially. Better? No, it was absolute, there was no choice allowed. And this same civilization paradoxically preserved at its very root a supreme instance of the other sort: better that one man should die for the people. . . .

The reappearance of the teams on the playing field caused Charles to break off at this place the thread of these somewhat elevated considerations. The captains advanced from either side to the center and there conferred with the referee. After this both sides lined up for the kick-off and stood to attention, along with the entire audience, while the national anthem was played by the band and metallically sung by a tenor voice.

The game then should have begun forthwith, but there was a further delay. A devout voice, on the same public address system, began to intone some species of prayer mixed with explanations, from all which Charles obscurely was able to gather that someone, a student, had somehow managed to fall into that bonfire last night at one or another stage of the proceedings, that this person had been terribly burned and taken to hospital, that he—or she, Charles did not catch the name—was on the critical list and might or might not live. The voice ended by suggesting a minute of silent prayer, and since no one in the stadium controverted the suggestion, that minute then followed, while the football players stood uneasily with bowed heads and held their helmets like extra heads in their hands. At the end of one minute exactly, the voice coughed and said "Amen." The Homecoming Game then began.

When it was over, when in the cold shadows of the coming dark small mobs of people tore down the goal posts, while others seemed to stray aimlessly over the torn battleground as though seeking something they had lost, when the great crowd migrated slowly through many gates and dispersed, moving with the sheepish, bewildered resignation of men and women wakened from a dream in which some sad and terrible truth has been revealed, which they are unable to interpret although they will soon reduce it to the practical commonplaces of their daily lives, Charles remained for a long time where he was. It may be, indeed, that he quite consciously savored and even sentimentalized a trifle the pathos of this moment which of all moments— in the darkening and scarred arena, when the heroes have gone home and human action has failed once again and the monks are singing on the steps of Ara Coeli—belonged to the historian's brand of elegiac poetry. This historian, however, had nothing to say just at present. He was uncertain as to the precise nature of what he had witnessed, and there he sat in the developing chill and gloom, while many slow figures moved and vanished before him and the great stone bowl grew very quiet.

As long as any action lay in the future, he reflected,

it belonged to freedom and seemed to be accountable to human decisions; as soon as that same action had become past, it looked not merely necessary with the necessity of what is plainly irrevocable, gone, dead, but as though it had always been necessary even before being enacted, and it appeared as though human wills had never affected the result, could never have affected the result, save in the way of making it more certain than ever of coming to pass; so that one inclined to bow the head and say, with a certain great master who was, however, romantically inclined in such things, *Ducunt fata volentem, nolentem trahunt.*

It had always been in the cards that things should fall just as they had fallen; nor could anyone ever *know* whether his actions or those of others had or could have affected the result. For it lay in the nature of time itself that the experimental method was impossible to be applied to human action; consequently the great lesson of necessity, even presuming it to be quite true, was precisely the lesson of all which could never be learned; must never be learned; to learn it was to die. Not to learn it, however, was as certainly to die, and perhaps the secular heroism presently available (to people, at least, of Charles Osman's quality and kind) was only this, to bear without despairing utterly the destructive nature of the truth as an element too cold by many degrees for human skin.

All the wisdom in this hullabaloo over the truth, however, consisted just in this, that the wake of all events reveals foolishness and sorrow and reason for repentance, if only for an instant before the waters close and we proceed in wisdom and faith once more; even at the moment of repentance our ship's prow is bravely cutting the unknown water ahead. A sorry predicament!—leading Charles Osman to exclaim inwardly, "If it were all to be done over again, I should have had to behave in exactly the same way." Which was as much as to say that the captain goes down with his ship, and must do so as a matter of form and human dignity, whether it sinks as a result of his own drunken folly, the incompetence of his officers and crew, or the stroke of lightning from heaven on a clear night.

It was a clear night, by now. Charles rose from his place and wearily left the stadium. Despite the brilliant performance of Ray Blent, who had played nearly the whole game and played it well, in Charles's opinion, even scoring once on the run-back of a punt, the home team had lost by a matter of three touchdowns, a point spread well in excess of the minimum said to have been guaranteed by certain shrewd and big-time gamblers. So that honesty by its utmost exertions had done what dishonesty would have done, and appearances and reality were mysteriously at one.

Charles thought, would have taken oath, that the boy for whom he had made himself responsible had played honestly; but the nature of things, in the result, made the point impossible to prove. Also, he had to allow, his own impression could not be regarded as expert; for all his nostalgic, nervous pleasure in the game of football he remained very much an amateur spectator, who watched the ball at all times (or tried to, even that could become difficult in a game at which deception had become the basis of style), who could never remember at the crucial instant, however often he had been told, to pay some heed to the line charging or to the block which might free the runner, and who might be thought to find all his love for the game in the inarticulate identification of his youthful self with every splendid and audacious action on the field. This identification, this empathic, mimetic clenching of the muscles and excitement of the heart prolonged over two hours while the golden sun fell behind the stadium wall, was doubtless responsible, along with the moral sadness of the business, for his present sense of being through, finished, drained of energy as, in a way, life itself seemed to have been drained of meaning.

Yet such feelings were not without some sort of consolation. It, whatever it was, at any rate was over. Charles stopped outside the gate and looked up at the black implacable bulk of the wall, at the stars, at the remaining band of pure, red-gold light in the west, outlining the hills. Autumn, football, the pale, clear, fictitious glory. Adolescent glory. But what would you put in its place? Football is unreal, if you care to say so; but as you grow older many things become unreal, and football stands out somehow as an image. And there under the shadow of the stone, empty stadium, after the captains and the kings depart, after all the others too depart, in that last lonely and cold air, you may, if you care for games, experience something of what is meant by vanished glory. Symbolical—perhaps. But it is commonly allowed that you may more easily call the things of this world symbolical than say what they are symbolical of.

Consoling as it had seemed in its immediacy, the idea that everything was finished proved hard to take, since it meant a finish without result. Yesterday's furious and meaningful (at the time) activity, inane as it had by now turned out to be, surely could not be allowed to end in this way, with Charles walking up and down in his small sitting room, alone except for the portrait of his dead wife, whose eyes seemed to follow him with a particular glittering constancy. He was chilled, hungry, tired, did not want to eat and did not believe he could sleep; after considering a trip down to the kitchen to make tea, he poured himself a drink instead, and carried the glass up and down the room with him.

It was clear to him at this time that everyone involved, having made use of him all day yesterday with an intensity that now looked absurd, would leave him strictly alone. He had a right to be angry, but doubted that he had the energy to be more than miserable. After all the heroics, dramatics, and noble expressions of principle, it was very inconvenient to have been more or less forced to resign over something which by no stretch of the imagination could be thought his fault; even the principle involved, whatever it was, seemed small, distant, and ridiculous. One would have to finish out the term, in any case, and possibly even the whole year, till June; that was no less a point of honor than a matter of contract, or no more.

Charles had resisted the wish to phone Lily in the late morning, in part because he felt she should phone him, in somewhat greater part because he thought, being sober and a trifle sickish, more about his age and dignity than he had the night before; now he suddenly phoned and learned that she was out, the speaker (a maid) did not know where. This was most unsatisfactory.

Turning from the phone, he faced the portrait on his desk, and something came back to him of last night's dream. He had been taking her body, in the coffin, back home for burial, but it was not much as it had been in waking life years ago. This was a matter of pushing the casket (on wheels) or (sometimes) driving it down long halls, past classrooms (his old high school, in fact), through the gym, the locker room, out over the football field (the small grandstand packed with people, boys and girls, his old classmates perhaps—but their faces were vague—waving money). The object was to bury the casket down at the far end zone, where it seemed a small stone house had been built for that very purpose, but the field was crowded with running players who would dance up to him eagerly and brush his legs with a pretense of tackling which though it never succeeded never failed of frightening.

Charles mentally turned away, having no wish to explore this matter any further. But recollection deepened despite him. The small stone house, when he reached it with his burden of responsibility, was quite large inside, an airy bedroom with curtains blowing in at the windows, white curtains. In the center of the bed lay Raymond Blent, or the stone image of him. "He wasn't invited," a voice said close by, and Charles began pushing that granite figure over to one side to make room on the bed for his wife's body. The cold, heavy sleeper did not move, and Charles woke up sweating (as with effort) and scared.

The thought now came to him, recalling all this, that Blent might kill himself. Rationally regarded, this was an absurd thought; nor was Charles a man to believe in prophetic dreams, generally speaking. This dream, however, had *come to him.* It compellingly seemed to want to say something to him, and all at once he felt that if one were reasonable—the very opposite of rationalistic—one could not avoid giving heed.

Come right down to it, was it so absurd? Did not students at this institution no less than at any other do away with themselves (or try to) at an average rate of, he had once been told, three or four in any academic year? Had not Blent tried it once himself? Had he not even said (yesterday, but it seemed ages ago) that if the game were lost he would do just that? More or less as a means of currying favor with Charles Osman, and getting back the good opinion he had forfeited by his error (or, more accurately, by the confession of it)? Like those Indian tribesmen Charles had once read of, who on suffering any indignity took their revenge by disemboweling themselves on the doorstep of the man who had wronged them.

Under the horrifying conviction borne by this idea Charles suddenly opened his door. Of course there was nothing outside. He faced again the eyes of his wife, and asked himself: do you wish for his death?

Be honest, he argued with his unwillingness, it would be vastly convenient. He had a momentary vision of himself and Lily Sayre standing hand in hand by the hero's grave.

Charles told himself that in the light of this vicious and inadmissible wish it became his duty to go find out, to go see, and, if possible, save. With the hope, possibly, of arriving just too late? Never. More likely one would find nothing whatever wrong and would suffer in consequence the most ridiculous embarrassment, since it was clearly not possible to say, I came by to see if by any remotest chance you had hung yourself from a coat-hook. There must be an excuse, then, and it would be this: I came by to find out if Miss Sayre (speaking very formally) told you that I managed last night to return the money and get you off the hook (but mind those metaphors, please).

Charles got out the College directory and learned that Raymond Blent lived in a boarding house located at the foot of College Hill. Very well, he would go there. It was an ambiguous index to the state of his mind that, though the errand might be thought to be either absolutely unnecessary or, if necessary, extremely urgent, he decided to walk, telling himself it was a matter of a few minutes' difference only and that he needed the time to calm himself.

The ten-minute walk, on the contrary, increased his nervous exasperation and a dreamy sense he had of the folly of this adventure, which was the sillier for being secret and never to be admitted to any other person. He walked fast, and began to feel terribly overheated, even feverish; perhaps he had caught cold sitting too long in that chilly stadium with its stone seats. And could it really be true, as he had been told many years ago, that one got piles from sitting on stone?

The boarding house proved to be one of a row of such dreary-looking places, run up during the expansion of the College, which had produced here a slum just as surely as would any other kind of factory. By the small light in the hall Charles made out that Blent lived on the second floor in the rear. The front door stood open; he rang the bell and went up.

He had knocked twice, with no response, before he became aware that two other people, a man and a woman, were sitting on the window sill down at the far end of the dark hall.

"Raymond isn't at home, it looks like," the man said, and the woman added, "Are you a friend of his? Does he expect you?"

They came forward uncertainly. Charles introduced himself and learned they were Blent's parents, but could not see much about them on account of the gloom.

"Raymond wrote me about you," the mother said. "He admires you very much, Mr. Osman."

"He was supposed to meet us here after the game," the man said glumly and with a great sigh of whisky which enveloped Charles for an instant and was gone.

"He doesn't answer?" A cold qualm touched Charles on the heart. "Maybe he hasn't got home yet, then," he said easily, though the game had ended some two hours ago.

"Let's go back and wait in the little restaurant, Lizzie," the man said. "This is the second time we come over," he added to Charles. "Between times we waited in that Mike's College Café at the end of the street."

"Where you had quite enough for one afternoon," said the woman.

"Maybe the Professor would join us?" Mr. Blent somewhat pleadingly suggested. "It's more comfortable than waiting in this hallway."

"I think I won't, thanks," said Charles. "I may take a walk and come back."

"We'll go, then," Mrs. Blent said, "but you'll have coffee this time."

When they were out the door downstairs Charles knocked again, and even listened at the door; he could hear nothing, and had the horrified thought of Blent's hanging on the other side of the wooden panel, two or three inches away.

Nonsense. He simply isn't in. If he were, though, how dreadful for the parents.

Charles went out and walked around the miserable neighborhood for precisely fifteen minutes, deliberately trying not to look back at the house (as though making every opportunity for the boy to be at home next time). If he had really promised to meet his folks after the game, that looked just a trifle sinister, did it not?

Charles mounted the stairs again and knocked. Nothing happened. The silence and darkness were disturbing enough by now, and with sudden decision he went downstairs to find the landlady, who had the front apartment on the ground floor.

The landlady, a neat grandmotherly sort of person

who however smelled strongly of beer, proved to be somewhat deaf. By an exchange of screams and gestures Charles was able to gather that she would not in any case have heard whether her tenant had come in or not. She seemed willing enough to get her keys and accompany him upstairs (by this time he had dismayed visions of having to call the police—"And what led you to suspect, Professor, that you might find the boy dead?"), but on the landing, after he knocked loudly without result, she seemed to grow obscurely suspicious of him, and refused to unlock the door.

"How do I know who you are?" she cried very loudly a number of times, and, "You might be anybody in the world, for all I know."

Charles was about to give up and go home when Blent's voice sounded from within.

"All right. All right. Just a minute."

This minute went by before a light showed itself under the door, which then flew open; there stood Blent, in shirt and trousers evidently put on in some haste.

"Oh, it's you," he said to the man who might be considered to be his benefactor, and then, a little more graciously, "Come in. I was just resting. I'm glad you're here."

The landlady went muttering down the stairs as Charles entered the room, shutting the door behind him. It was dismally a student's room, with a sad desk and blotter and a few thick library books; a half-open closet door showed a heap of dirty laundry inside; another door evidently led to the bedroom.

"I wanted to see you," Blent said, "to give you this. It was under the door when I got home."

He handed Charles a thick Manila envelope, portfolio size; this was full of bills.

"I counted it," Blent said resignedly. "Fifteen hundred. I played an honest game, sir. I wish you'd take all that and put it wherever you put the other lot."

Charles finally found something to say.

"Didn't Lily—didn't Miss Sayre tell you I gave that money back? At least," he added, holding the envelope in both hands, "I thought I did."

Blent apparently misinterpreted his frown.

"Look, Mr. Osman," he said sternly, "I played as hard as I could. We just didn't get going, that's all, it happens to a team sometimes. But I wasn't playing to lose. If I had been, would I be giving you the money? You would never have got to know about the money."

"It's not your honesty I'm thinking about," Charles said. "Miss Sayre didn't phone you this morning?"

"No, sir."

"You might as well keep the money," Charles said, on the point by now of resigning from everything. "In a way you've earned it—oh, not by dishonesty, I don't mean that. I only mean that by now it's impossible to figure out who it belongs to if not to you."

"Well, I won't take it," said Blent severely. "I know what you think of me—you'd like to see me take it, then you'd be justified. Deep down, you really still think I'm crooked. I won't take it, sir. Don't think I'm not grateful, but you did make it your responsibility, the money, didn't you? You can see I can't take it back."

226

"Yes, I suppose you can't," Charles wearily agreed. "You played a good game, I thought. I don't believe you're crooked, and I take back what I said before you left yesterday. I'm sorry for having said it, and now I'd as soon forget the whole stupid business—but what about this?" He held out the envelope.

Blent suddenly said, "I know you're thinking of what I said about killing myself if we lost—don't you worry about me, sir, that was a silly thing to say, but I guess I was upset. After all," he added, "I've learned this much—it is only a game."

"After all," Charles repeated in a bemused way. There was a knock at the door, and Blent opened it to his mother and father.

There were greetings all around. Blent seemed both reserved and nervous in the presence of his parents; he kept telling them to wait downstairs for five minutes.

"I'll be with you just as soon as I can," he said.

The father, who clearly had not been drinking coffee after all, said, "I just want you to know, Ray, we're getting back together, Mother and I. We were proud of you, Son, today, and—"

"We'll talk about it later," the mother said with a glance at Charles. "Ray has something to discuss with his teacher. You and I will just wait downstairs—no, not in that café," she was saying as they left, "but right downstairs."

"That's just dandy," Blent said to Charles when they had gone. "It's the third time they've got back together."

The slam of the door having produced the false impression, probably, that all the guests had left, the bed-room door opened and Lily appeared, dressed in a bath-robe much too large for her. On seeing Charles she stopped, made as if to return to the bedroom, realized it was now too late, and came fully forth.

"Oh, dear," she said, and had the grace at least not to smile.

Raymond Blent responded to this with a kind of helpless but cinematic urbanity.

"I think you two have met," he said, blushing with pride or shame or both. "I hope, sir," he continued, "you'll overlook the rules, you know, about women in the rooms, but Miss Sayre and I are going to get married."

Charles abruptly and in spite of himself laughed, or at least made a sound like "tee hee." This silly noise lingered in the room for a long moment, until Charles rapidly fled, slamming the door behind him and getting fully downstairs and into the street before noticing that he held all that money in its envelope, rather delicately clutched in both hands as one might hold a prayerbook.

3

Charles walked all the way into town to the Aaron Burr, under the odd impression that he would get there faster if he kept going than if he took time out at some gas station or diner to phone a cab. By the time he arrived he was in a high sweat, disheveled, glowing with ill-health. Mr. Giardineri thought he might be drunk, but could not be certain; at any rate, when he had got

Charles away from the bar, where numerous celebrants of both colleges had begun to look piercingly at him, and back into his own office, he took a chance and poured them each a fat glass of whisky.

"Someone has blundered," Charles said, waving that envelope about somewhat wildly. "Mine not to reason why—yours to reason why." He banged the envelope down across the desk and money slid out of its open mouth. "Honesty forever, as I am an Eagle Scout." He drank some of the whisky and wiped his mouth. "I'm awfully tired, though," he added.

"Now relax, Professor," Giardineri said. "You've got a right to be a little peeved, but relax, there's nothing that can't be explained."

"That's what I thought once," said Charles inconsequently.

"Everything I did," Giardineri said, "I did to protect you, and protect the College—and me too, of course. I've always been a good friend of the College, Dr. Osman, everybody knows that's so."

"I didn't say you weren't, did I?" muttered Charles.

"There will always be gambling," the innkeeper said impressively, "and where there is gambling there will always be dishonesty. No professor could ever change that. Things are the way they are, that's all."

"I grant your major," said Charles, but Giardineri disregarded this and went on.

"I didn't want you to get into trouble, Dr. Osman. I've always thought you were a very nice young fellow, and probably very bright, too, about school stuff, whatever it is you teach—but a little innocent, if you get what

229

I mean. A little simple where the real world's concerned. I had to kind of short-circuit you, and keep everything in the family."

"I don't know what you mean."

"You won't like it, either, when you know," the other said, "and I can't blame you. But I've always valued my honesty too, Professor—it's the thing a man in business has got to have if he doesn't have anything else. Even brains he can get on without, but he must be honest. So I've got to give you the straight story even if you get sore.

"You never met any gambler, Doc. Max was a busboy of mine off-duty; you might have recognized him but I didn't have a chance to get anybody else, and people don't usually recognize busboys. Now wait, before you get all overheated—he didn't promise you anything, did he?"

"No," Charles admitted.

"He better not have," said Giardineri emphatically, "he was told not to. I figured, see, we'd just hold on to the dough till the game was over—"

"I owe you five dollars, that reminds me." Charles gestured toward the money on the desk. "Take it out of that."

"Forget it, Doc. You never had any chance. I told you I didn't want your money. That game was in the bag before it started."

"Not if I returned that five hundred it wasn't."

"You wouldn't be so hot at business, Professor," Mr. Giardineri said. "You don't think those boys would leave the fix to one player, do you? What kind of policy

230

would that be? Suppose he got sick or ineligible, or re-
pentant like your player did? If you ever fix something
you've got to go all the way and see that it stays fixed.
Anyhow, backs are shaky people to deal with, they're
nervous, they're full of cheap heroics—guards and
tackles can do more for you and do it quieter and
they generally don't have such high ideals. See what
I mean?"

As this appalling news sank in Charles giggled a
little and allowed he saw what Mr. Giardineri meant.

"So even if you returned the money it wouldn't have
made any difference—except one difference, maybe: it
would have got some hard people sore at me, which
would be bad for business, not to mention health."

Smiling, Mr. Giardineri folded the money back in
its envelope and pushed it across the desk.

"So you're in some bucks, Professor, what's so terrible
about that? It come from crooks, and they don't even
know they lost it. They're probably so loaded right now
they'd give that amount to a waiter after dinner. And
another thing—"

He took the other envelope from a desk drawer.

"I got to thinking, while we had the five hundred
around the house just picking up dust, why not let it
earn its keep? So I put it on the other team for you."

Charles stared at him and could say nothing. Giardineri pushed this envelope in turn over the desk.

"One thousand," he said easily, "to make up a little
for my having to play it deep and dirty on you. I'm
sorry it isn't more, but it was too late to get better than
even money."

Charles got his wits about him enough to say, "You keep the profits anyhow."

"Don't you worry about me, Dr. Osman," Giardineri said. "I did all right on the game. I'll do this, though, I'll take your five out of this, then let's shake hands and call it square, right?"

Elaborately, like a magician being aboveboard, he extracted a twenty-dollar bill and put three fives in its place. Then he got up, and Charles did too.

"Now another thing, Doctor," Giardineri said, holding out his hand, which Charles mechanically accepted, "you look starved. Go in the dining room and have dinner, it's all on the house. Better not drink much more, though. You look—tired, sort of." He clapped Charles heartily on the back and began to escort him out through the bar. "Try the Lobster Aaron Burr," he whispered conspiratorially. "I made it myself."

Max the busboy passed before them carrying a loaded tray of dirty dishes and not looking at Charles, who stopped in his tracks and began to laugh, a loud, cracked, uncontrollable kind of laughter which did not sound altogether rational. Mr. Giardineri sighed.

"Maybe on second thought, it's not dinner you need," he said. "Come on along, now." With unembarrassed patience, gentleness and courtesy, gathering Charles's hat and coat on the way, he escorted him out the front door. If people stared, Mr. Giardineri stared back.

"Frank," he said to the doorman, "take my car and run Mr. Osman out to the College. He'll tell you where he lives."

The doorman tipped his cap smartly and went for the car. Mr. Giardineri waited with Charles.

"You're a little sick maybe?" he said. "Do you want me to go with you?"

"Very good of you," Charles managed to say, "but never mind."

"The money's in your overcoat pocket," Giardineri whispered as the car drove up and he bundled Charles into the back.

The money's in my overcoat pocket, said Charles to himself as the car, a Cadillac it was, hummed along. He felt in his pocket and there it was, there they both were, the two envelopes. Money, which everyone tried so hard to get, suddenly began to seem a commodity impossible ever to get rid of; perhaps it would soon take to growing in the fields until there was no more grain, but only money.

When the doorman asked him where he wanted to be driven, Charles on an impulse directed him to Leon Solomon's house, where he got out, thanked the man and offered from one of those envelopes the first bill that came up, a twenty.

"That's not necessary, sir," Frank said. "This is a favor from the boss. Anyhow—do you teach out here?"

"Yes," Charles said.

"I make more than you do, then," Frank said. "Save your dough." And he drove away.

Charles climbed the steps and rang the bell.

"Lord, you look awful," said Leon Solomon. "Come in the house."

"Something I've come for," Charles said. "Special errand." He allowed himself to be led inside to the living room, which tonight, curiously, was fresh and clean. Leon tried to take his coat, but Charles, hands in pockets, clutched it around him; indeed he seemed to have a chill and was shuddering a bit. Leon made him sit on the couch.

"Are you drunk?" he asked. "Can I get you anything? Here, lie down." Charles passively accepted this attention too, and heard Leon in the kitchen telling Myra to make coffee. A moment later he was back with a blanket, which he placed carefully over Charles.

"There, now, take it easy for a minute," he said, "and tell me what's on your mind."

Myra came into the room and stood in the doorway. She was smiling. Charles had never seen her smile before, and considered it greatly improved her looks.

"Coffee in a few minutes," she said. "You do look sick."

Charles, wrestling with blanket and coat, managed to sit up and draw forth the two envelopes.

"I don't want any false pride from you, from either of you," he said, "and I'll not go into what we historians call the provenience of this wretched stuff—" spilling the money out on the floor— "but here is a little gift."

He sank back on the couch and watched with some pleasure the stupefying effect of his gesture.

"Don't think it's charity," he said. "It's only justice. You are the ones who suffered the most, and this wad comes to you by courtesy of civilization itself and the nature of things as they are." Somewhat embarrassed then by their expressions, he added, "Think that it is for the children. It'll help if you don't get another job right away."

Myra got down on her knees and began carefully to sweep all the bills up together.

"It's very good of you," Leon slowly began. "Of course, I couldn't take it anyhow—"

"Nonsense, nonsense," said Charles with feeble avuncular heartiness.

"But you don't know yet—I tried to phone you—you don't know that the situation has changed—again."

"Changed, how?"

"I'm back on the team, I guess you might say," Leon continued. "Nagel came round to apologize after the game."

"After the game?"

"Well, yes. I gather we lost. I'm not sure he would have done it otherwise, since then he might have felt more justified. But he came in about five-thirty, and was very nice. He apologized personally, he apologized for the College, he as good as apologized for the board of trustees and the government of the country; I think he even vaguely said something about world Protestantism, too."

"So now you're unresigned?" said Charles.

"After last night, I guess, and after losing the game— he told me it was 'only a game'—he figured the handsome thing was the best thing, since if all that ever got out it'd sound like there had been a pogrom up here; so I get a raise, he said, a bonus for now and a regular raise for next year; next meeting of the trustees he recommends me for associate professor; I've got tenure; everything is sweetness and light. So you can see," Leon concluded, "I don't need the money. But I wouldn't have taken it anyhow."

"But you took it from Nagel?"

"Well, Charles, that's a very different thing, a kind of vindication."

"And about politics, your misspent youth, and all that?"

"I told him what I told you, and he took it. He said if I spoke to the committee that way he'd see to it there was no more trouble."

Charles lay back and considered this in silence. Myra had the money back in one envelope, the large one, which she placed on his lap.

"So now it seems I'm the only one on the outside," he said at last, sighing.

"You know that needn't be so," Leon pointed out. "He's just as anxious to apologize to you as to me."

"Seems you changed your mind about things awful fast," said Charles with a hint of anger.

"Ah, you convinced me," Leon said, "and of course Myra did too. Why go on fighting that hopeless battle all alone? We don't live that way any more, in this country. We might as well get our share while prosperity lasts. I owe it to the kids."

"So," said Charles, leaning on one elbow. Leon got nervous under his stare.

"I tried to phone you," he said, "but you were out."

Myra brought in the coffee and cups on a tray; Charles refused his.

"I don't mean to be unfriendly," he said. "I feel sick to my stomach, that's all." The moral implication, however cravenly expressed, was not lost on Leon.

"If you think I'm doing wrong, Charles," he said, "say so. Would you advise me to resign again, for good, as a matter of principle? I can see the point of it, if that's what you want."

Charles looked at him steadily.

"No," he said after a minute, "I'm about through making recommendations for other people's behavior. About the only advice I have left," he added with a pained smile, "is to disregard any advice I might give."

"I don't deny my conscience feels a little itchy," Leon insisted. "I told Nagel that, too. I said I wanted it clearly understood that his behavior was expedience and nothing else, purely, you might say, technical and procedural, but that I was too tired and beat to do any more resisting, ever. I said he was lucky to be able to flannel things over this time, and that I was conniving at it for my own profit, but at least, I said, there was no point in anybody's deceiving himself.

"I told him, too," Leon continued, "that he was like the ship's captain whom Socrates talks about in the *Gorgias*, who does his best for people in his own technical area, sailing the ship, but has the wit to realize he can't know whether he's done 'em good or harm. You know," he added, "there's a moral in that for you too, Charles. Let me read you the place; it won't take a minute."

He picked up a volume which had been lying open and face down on the mantel.

"Socrates has been saying that navigation is important because it saves people from the perils of the sea just as rhetoric saves them from the perils of the law. For doing this service, he says, the captain does not give himself grand airs but simply charges a small fee; and he tells how this captain, after landing the passengers safely, walks the shore in a modest manner. 'For he knows, I guess, how to estimate the uncertainty as to which of his passengers he has benefited by not letting them be lost as sea, and which he has injured, being aware that he has put them on shore not a bit better than when they came aboard, either in body or in soul.'"

Leon looked up from the book.

"It goes on in that strain," he said, "and it ends, as I told Nagel, 'This is why it is not the custom for the pilot to give himself grand airs.'"

"Am I like that?" Charles asked after a silence.

"I mean, you're like what it talks about—it applies to you, maybe in a number of ways. You tried to do things for people, but unlike the captain you tried to decide what would be best for them, and this was a matter outside your technical competence. I honor the ideal, Charles, for it was mine as well; but you failed, you would always fail."

"How sad," said Charles, "and especially for Socrates. What about the just man?"

"These days," Leon heavily replied, "everything is too complicated for the just man to keep track of."

"So we're all technicians," Charles said, getting up. "Philosophy mechanics, history mechanics, lab assistants to vanished scientists, apprentices without a sorcerer and the water already beginning to spill over the bucket's edge."

He stuffed the envelope back into his pocket and started toward the door.

"One more technical operation," he said, "and I think I'm through. Leon, I'm afraid you're right," and he added, rather wistfully, "Curse God and die."

"I see what you mean," Leon said. "I do see what you mean. You're not angry?"

"No, I'm not," Charles said, and they shook hands. "I'm not absolutely sure what I am. Good night, both of you." And so he went out.

4

President Nagel drew Charles into the house.

"Delighted you came, delighted," he said. "I phoned your house twice, you weren't there. Come—in the study—we have guests. We almost always have guests," he added wearily.

Once in the study he turned to look at Charles closely, under a good light.

"You ought to be in bed," he said. "You don't look well at all. Here, sit down, and let me bring you something to drink. Or maybe you'd like a nice hot cup of tea?"

Charles said he thought he would rather have a touch of whisky straight. Dr. Nagel brought this from a stand in the corner, and they sat down in opposed easy chairs at either side of the grate where a small logfire was burning.

Dr. Nagel said, "I behaved badly last night, Charles,

and I want to apologize for that before you say anything." He fell silent for a moment and stared into the fire.

"That student died," he said, "the boy who got burned last night. I was just on the phone to his parents. Awful, awful.

"I've always considered myself a practicing Christian, Charles," he said gravely, and went on, fortunately, before Charles, who was perhaps a trifle delirious, could ask whether practice made perfect, "but sometimes I feel things are much too much for me. I was wrong ever to become an administrator. I should have remained a teacher. I think I was a good teacher, but who knows about that? Anyhow—last night was dreadful, and I hope I am ashamed of myself, and not merely of the fact that you saw me as I was."

"I can't blame you," Charles said, and added, "Nobody can blame anybody."

"I gave way before power," Nagel continued, "and then I used my own tiny power to cover it up that I had done so. Charles, do you think I should resign the presidency?"

"I'm sorry," Charles said, "but I'm not in the advice business any more."

They were silent for a moment.

"You know, I probably won't," the President said. "I know myself that well. Perhaps I shall pretend I'm going to for a while, but at last I won't. If you would tell me to, though, I would," he added.

"I can't tell you anything of that nature, and you know it."

Dr. Nagel sighed, perhaps with relief.

"You won't resign either, Charles." It was a flat statement.

"Why not?"

"We've both of us gone too far. We've taken the King's shilling, so to say, we're in. Look, if you weren't here you'd be elsewhere, wouldn't you?"

"Impeccable logic."

"Elsewhere there would be football teams too, wouldn't there?"

"You needn't carry on so," Charles said grumpily, "I concede the whole argument, but I might just resign anyhow, to be absurd."

"I've reinstated Mr. Solomon, he has accepted my apologies—it removes the cause of your resignation."

"Yes, I know that."

"Then you know, don't you, that in some odd way we've squeaked through—this time? We were lucky, no permanent damage is done—"

"Except for one burned student."

"Please don't be frivolous, Charles. I take that very seriously. Very seriously. But it was an accident, it had nothing to do with the situation."

"Symbolical," said Charles owlishly, "symbolical."

"No permanent damage, for all our folly. We lost the game, but after all it's only a game, and there will be other games."

"Which reminds me," Charles said. His coat lay on the floor next to his chair, and from it he drew forth once again that envelope.

"I want to establish," he said importantly, "a football scholarship, in the name of Raymond Blent. The principal may be used until it is gone for the purpose of buying the best high-school back available—if twenty-five hundred is enough."

They stared at one another for a moment. The President waved the money away.

"You know I won't take that, Charles," he said. "It is a clownish gesture you're making, and on your pay you can't afford it."

"My pay?" Charles laughed and then said, "Do you want to know where this money comes from?"

The President said, "I suppose that means you want to tell me. Tell, then, if you must."

"It comes out of the nowhere into the here," said Charles. "I don't know, as a matter of fact, where it comes from. It represents, though, the amount which one fine young athlete was to take in consideration of our losing the game."

"Was to take? But he didn't then, since you have the money." The President cautiously added, "You mean Raymond Blent?"

"I mentioned no names," said Charles, "and anyhow, as you say, he didn't. I gather, though, that others did."

"Charles, have you any evidence at all of that?"

"No, not a bit, nothing."

"Then you shouldn't say it."

"Do you believe me when I say it, Harmon?"

The President took a long time over this, and finally said, "Yes, I do. What can be done, Charles?"

"Not a thing, not a single blessed thing," Charles

replied, "unless you want to accept my football scholarship. On second thought," he added, "why don't I put it in my own name?"

"Charles, I've said I won't consider that," said Dr. Nagel, helplessly spreading his hands. "I can't. You know, I've nothing to do with all that, officially I don't know about it; football here is an amateur sport."

"What do I do with it, then?"

"Keep it," said Nagel earnestly. "That's my advice. Lord knows you did enough for it."

"Hah," said Charles. "How shall I report it on my tax return?"

"Keep it under the mattress," said Nagel, "keep it anywhere, how should I know? If you like, call it a grant from the College—for research into the nature of history."

Charles had nothing to say to this. He drank his whisky.

"Are you going to marry Herman's daughter?" Nagel asked. "Was that the truth?"

"No," Charles said, and added, "Uriah came back."

"What does that mean? Oh—I understand, I think." He coughed, and said pompously, "May I understand, Dr. Osman, that you will retain your position here on the faculty?"

"Oh, I guess so," Charles said crossly. "I don't know any longer what the squabble is about, or was. Everybody seems to've won something out of the deal. Blent got his girl, I've got money, a kind of bride-price as you might say, the people back of it all have got

243

enormous sums of money, probably, and you have your college. Even Blent's parents are going to live together again. What should I be," he added, "but a teacher of history?"

"You know," the President said, "it's odd how things come right, Charles. Like the British, we muddle through—"

"Into the valley of death," muttered Charles.

"—for all our folly and criminal stupidity and dreadful self-interest, we've come through, and it seems as if everyone were happier—or better off, anyhow—than before. It reminds me, Charles, if you'll allow an old teacher to be professional, it reminds me of something Socrates said in the *Gorgias*, about the old ship's captain walking up and down the shore—"

But Charles had begun to laugh uncontrollably, and could not stop for a couple of minutes.

"You are an old fake," he finally brought out, and there was a silence.

"Oh, you know about the ship's captain, do you?" Harmon Nagel paused. "Yes, I am an old fake," he finally said. "I don't know what else it's possible to be. Here the whole world is likely to fly into a million pieces any day, and meanwhile everybody is making more and more money. I don't know anyone who can change it—or anyone who would dare change it if he could."

A few minutes later he saw Charles to the door, offering to drive him home.

"I'd rather walk, thanks."

"Well—take care of yourself. Go straight to bed when

you get in. You've got a bad chill coming on, if nothing worse."

They said good night, and Charles started up the street toward his rooms.

So it seemed that after all the fuss nothing much had happened, he thought, as he passed slowly from streetlamp to streetlamp, entering and leaving the cold, glowing areas of light as if moving in some very simple form of checker game. His head ached, he had a fever, he did indeed feel chilled; by morning a severe cold was predictable, if nothing worse.

In this condition it came to him to begin tearing up all that money slowly and carefully and leaving behind him a paper trail as he walked on and on, past his home, out of the region of the College forever, up into the dark hills beyond—forever. It would make a splendid legend: Mad Historian Leaves Money. Hounds Follow As Hare Outruns Cash.

He actually began to do this, taking the first twenty-dollar bill and beginning slowly to tear it in strips. He walked slowly on, scattering these fragments as he went.

"Hey, you there—" a loud voice followed him. "Hey, stop. Oh, Professor Osman."

It was the old campus policeman, Henry, who touched his cap politely but stood in his way.

"Your pockets got holes, Professor?" he asked genially. "Here, I'll help you." And he went down on hands and knees and began picking up those fragments of money. Charles helplessly watched.

"I got all I could find," the man said, coming back. "How did it get torn up, sir?" he asked, sternly suspicious though courteous. "I think, Professor," he added, "you maybe had enough party for tonight. I'll see you along to your house, if you like."

"Henry, you're a very sympathetic fellow," said Charles.

"You have to have sympathy in my business," Henry replied. "Human sympathy does more to keep people out of trouble than anything—than this, for instance," patting his night-stick.

Charles looked severely at him.

"Sympathy," he said with great and pedantic care, "sympathy, Henry, is the quality which makes us share with those less wise than ourselves the delusions which they are on the point of outgrowing. You need not see me home, thank you very much. Good night."

And he walked on, feeling however that Henry followed at a respectful distance.

Arrived home, he threw all that money on the desk. He was having a severe chill, certainly, but before retiring he took time to make himself a hot drink of Ovaltine, which he took to bed. Tomorrow, given sufficient health, he must prepare his future classes, on the end of Charles (of England), his brother's brief succeeding reign, and the Glorious Revolution (of 1688). Meanwhile, though he was shuddering terribly, he thought there was nothing wrong with him that Ovaltine would not cure, provided he drank it with the exemplary cheerfulness, courage, and constancy displayed by Socrates when they brought him the hemlock.

AFTERWORD

by *Albert Lebowitz*

Some years ago, in a kinder and gentler world of a benevolent ozone layer, Howard Nemerov and I played tennis under a hot St. Louis sun, at the public courts in University City's Heman Park. Our styles were very different. I was the self-taught player with coarse, eccentric strokes, unpredictable in speed and direction. Howard had, I am told by his widow, Peggy, received lessons early from a Davis Cup professional and stroked smoothly and elegantly. Only my single distinct advantage allowed our winnings to be divided equally; I was eager, in fact frenetically so, to run for every ball, while Howard sauntered around one spot on the court. His racquet, seeming to acquire preternatural extension, firmly and steadily as a baseball pitching machine, rifled my hard-earned shots back at me. When one of my returns proved to be out of reach, Howard would smile indulgently, shrug, and let it go, as if to say, it isn't whether you win or lose, but how much effort you must expend before remembering it's just a game. It occurred to me then as it does now that Howard dearly loved games because he refused, against all conventional wisdom, to take them seriously, to be a fanatic.

We played chess to much the same rhythms. Howard would glance casually at the board and make his move. I would sit stubbornly for minutes (we had no timer) while Howard would roam about the room, sometimes drinking his martini, other times softly whistling. We broke even at this game too.

Upon rereading *The Homecoming Game*, I was dazzled once again by the elegant economy of Howard's strokes. According to *A Journal of the Fictive Life*, Nemerov wrote the larger part of the novel in about a month, yet it emerges as a complex, tightly knit testimonial to the inevitable collapse into triviality of "moral" and other "life-and-death" human contests. Henry James speaks with reverence of Joseph Conrad's ability, through a multiplicity of narrators, to "do a thing that shall make it undergo most doing." In *The Homecoming Game*, given its single muted voice of Charles Osman, Associate Professor of History at the "College," Nemerov manages, nevertheless, to devise his own method of doing the "thing that shall make it undergo most doing": he creates a multiplicity of what may be termed "magic boxes," and proceeds not unlike a stage magician with rabbits up his sleeve. Festooned with Nemerovian wit and sparkle, loaded with such vital concerns as truth, morality, justice, and integrity, each of the boxes, upon being opened, proves to be replaced by another concern equally subject to transmogrification.

Nemerov opens the show by displaying the initial contents of his magic box; they appear, somewhat disappointingly, to be the too familiar bric-a-brac of a conventional morality play. The College's football homecoming game is imminent and not to be taken lightly, yet Professor Osman has flunked Raymond Blent, the star of the team, and rendered him ineligible to play. This crisis invites a gaggle of supplicants into Osman's life, initially ranging from vaguely menacing students, a blunt and loud Head of the Department, and Blent's fiancée, Lily Sayre (too attractive for Osman's good). Osman, as a prince of faith, should, of course, risk his career, perhaps life and limb, to preserve his integrity, despite being threatened by student Lou da Silva and, more, beguiled by the lovely Lily Sayre, who informs him that Blent deliberately flunked Osman's exam because she had given "back the pin." Lily says coolly, "our hero had made up his mind . . . and gave me to understand . . . that unless I restored the status quo nothing was worth while to him, he was going to give up and 'quit everything.' "

Osman muses, "To gain your good opinion, I should call the boy in, give him a quick make-up exam, and pass him if he doesn't know one Cromwell from the other?"

"Yes," she says earnestly. "Exactly that. Get him out there, give him back his football—push it into his arms if necessary and tell him to run with it. Make him understand that no romantic nonsense is to be tolerated. . . . What I want of you may be immoral, I know that, but it is ethical—it's the only honest way."

Lily leaves and her place is taken by the raw but subtly exercised power of Harmon Nagel, President of the College, a man who tries to be decent and honorable but, as he explains to Osman, is under his own pressures:

"A college president is in much the same situation as the prince Machiavelli described. . . . He rules 'his people,' that is, the students . . . he is a little remote and inaccessible and mysterious because he is not merely authority, he is the principle of authority embodied and made visible. . . . But it is the nobility—his faculty—and the courtiers—his administration—from whom he has most to gain and most to fear. The great robber barons of Sociology, English, the Physical

Sciences . . . you follow me? . . . Then, beyond all that, there are alumni and trustees . . . and yet the prince must keep his balance, and if possible even his dignity, among all those forces."

"We've got upper and nether millstones," said Charles, "if that's what you're trying to tell me. And if you mean that my failing Blent has put you under pressure, well, I'm sorry."

What will Osman as prince of faith do? We sigh a little at the predictability of it: even if he destroys himself, our hero will never yield to venal and demeaning considerations. Happily, we soon discover that this is not a stereotypical morality play at all, and that Nemerov is not interested in morality but in sleight of hand. Osman hasn't reckoned with a creator who finds both princes and ultimate faiths amusing and quite absurd. Our morality play vanishes with a flourish of black cape; Nemerov opens the box to reveal football coach Hardy, who alerts Osman to the fact that his moral dilemma may have disappeared; the football star has also failed the course of Leon Solomon, a true believer, an ideologist of the first rank, with, as a born loser, nothing to lose. Solomon and Osman were, as Osman put it, "intimately opposed":

They were just about of an age, but Solomon was a failure, one of those persons who for various reasons move from college to college without ever getting any where, a kind of academic tramp. . . . Solomon was Jewish. Charles was Jewish. . . . But even here, in the likeness, there was a strong element of difference. Leon Solomon was a New York Jew. Charles winced at having to put the matter so plainly even to himself. Charles on the other hand, laughable as the distinction might appear, was a Connecticut Jew . . . of the small town, inland variety which resembled the Connecticut Yankee at least a good deal more than it did the Jew, whether rich or poor, of New York City. Charles [unlike Solomon] did not look at all like the stereotype of a Jew.

Solomon gives way to the All-American hero, Raymond Blent, who confesses that he flunked the classes deliberately, not from unrequited love of Lily, but from the desire to escape the consequences of having accepted a bribe to throw the game. Even this seemingly definitive resolution of Osman's moral crisis is dismissed with a wave of the hand by the discovery that whether Raymond Blent played or not was immaterial since other pivotal members of the team have also been bribed.

Ultimately, even love and money, those passions that spin most plots, are trivialized. Osman relinquishes the idea of marrying Lily as easily and instantly as it first occurred to him. He winds up with Blent's fifteen hundred dollars of bribe money, and can't give it away, to Solomon, to the college, to anyone. He can't even, in a gesture reminiscent of Stanley Elkin's memorable story "I Look Out for Ed Wolfe," however hard he tries, throw it away. Elkin's Ed Wolfe *could* throw away his money precisely because, unlike Osman, he cared for it.

I venture the opinion that *The Homecoming Game* was as close to an autobiography as Howard ever got. Indeed, Howard was a Jewish professor, for many years at "an old, Eastern college. With respect to both adjectives, it was on the edge, but the old and eastern edge." He looked and acted more like a Connecticut Yankee than a New York Jew. He never quite abandoned "a sense of the mystery of authority, such a sense as everyone gets on being summoned to the principal's office for the first

251

time, and as some people never lose thereafter." (I once asked him whether he thought Bill Danforth, Chancellor of Washington University, a man Howard admired, respected, and liked, was anything like Harmon Nagel, the President of the College. Howard seemed somewhat amused and, after a moment, said simply, "Bill is a gentleman.") Much like Osman, if Howard had a moral philosophy, it was resistance to being bullied—by people, by dogmas.

We come to realize that Nemerov makes game of moral and intellectual problems in order *not* to trivialize them, solving them, closing them down. He honors their ambivalence and freedom from our control. Each new revelation in *The Homecoming Game* reminds us of the many possible ways there are of conceiving a problem that has a life of its own beyond the imperative of plot. Our relentless desire for resolutions, metaphorized in the endgames we play, is put in its place as merely a spur to the multiple curious ways of imagining how things might turn out. This converts fate into a sufficiency of satisfaction: we can smile indulgently at all the tennis balls that inevitably fall beyond our reach.

Howard Nemerov died on July 5, 1991. I trust and pray that he, as much as we continue to enjoy his work in all its wondrous variety, is taking his typically wry pleasure in the ultimate homecoming game.

ABOUT THE AUTHOR

Until his death on July 5, 1991, Howard Nemerov held the position of Edward Mallinckrodt Distinguished University Professor of English at Washington University in St. Louis. His illustrious career as a teacher began in 1946, when he left the Royal Canadian Air Force to teach World War II veterans about literature at Hamilton College in New York. After a long tenure at Bennington College and a shorter one at Brandeis University, Nemerov joined the faculty at Washington University in 1969.

Nemerov was a member of the American Academy of Arts and Letters and a fellow of the Academy of American Poets and of the American Academy of Arts and Sciences. Among the dozens of awards he received are the National Book Award (1978), the Pulitzer Prize for Poetry (1978), the Bollingen Prize for Poetry (1981), and the National Medal for the Arts in Poetry (1987).

From 1963 to 1964, Nemerov served as Consultant in Poetry to the Library of Congress, and when that post was elevated to that of Poet Laureate of the United States he again served, this time as the nation's third Poet Laureate, from 1988 to 1990.

The author of over three dozen works of fiction, poetry, and criticism, Howard Nemerov is one of America's most distinguished men of letters.